EVERY WITCH WAY

Nessa hates her full name — Agnes — which she inherited from her great-great-grandmother . . . but is that *all* she inherited? Because rumour had it that Great-great-granny Agnes was a witch, and a few unusual things have been happening to Nessa recently. First, there's the strange book she finds in her local coffee shop, and then the invite from her next-door neighbour Ewan Grainger to accompany him on a rather supernatural research trip. What ensues is a Halloween journey through Scotland in a yellow camper van, with just a touch of magic!

KIRSTY FERRY

EVERY WITCH WAY

Complete and Unabridged

LINFORD
Leicester

First published in Great Britain in 2017
Choc Lit Limited
Surrey

First Linford Edition
published 2018
by arrangement with
Choc Lit Limited
Surrey

A catalogue record for this book is available from the British Library.

ISBN 978–1–4448–3873–2

Published by
F. A. Thorpe (Publishing)
Anstey, Leicestershire

Set by Words & Graphics Ltd.
Anstey, Leicestershire
Printed and bound in Great Britain by
T. J. International Ltd., Padstow, Cornwall

This book is printed on acid-free paper

To all the 'singular animals' I've known and loved over the years. Some of you crossed the Rainbow Bridge a while ago, but you're always with me: our dogs Kim, Flint, Ayla and Polly; Flossie the cat; and Peter, my lovely budgie. With big 'woofs', of course, to Robbie — our current family furball!

Acknowledgements

Thank you to everybody who made this novella possible — and that includes my friend Hilary Kerr, who owned a real-life 'Winnie Bago' and very kindly allowed me to pilfer Winnie's name for Nessa's camper van! Thanks also to Geoff Holder, a very helpful chap who does exist and who did write the book *Maggie Wall — The Witch Who Never Was*. It's a fascinating read and a fascinating monument, and Geoff didn't seem to mind a random enquiry from me via his website when I began to research this story. I'd originally seen a photograph of Maggie's monument — in fact, it came from Hilary — and she said, 'Kirsty, you need to use this in one of your books!' I said, 'Ooh, thank you!' and stuck it on my Pinterest board whilst I pondered it.

When I'd finished my 'Rossetti Mysteries' series, I decided I fancied writing something a little bit different, and kept thinking about that monument. Then Nessa and Schubert burst into life from somewhere within my imagination and they seemed the perfect, quirky candidates to match with Maggie's monument. And because I do like a bit of the paranormal, I just had to follow the witchy angle through. Thank you again to everyone at Choc Lit who helped bring this little book, my first romcom, to life — thanks to the Tasting Panel who loved Nessa and Schubert as much as I did (especially Sam E, Sue R, Cindy T, Robyn K, Lisa B, Tricia R, Linda S, Kim R, Lisa B and Catherine L who passed the manuscript), to my editor, to my cover designer and to all the wider Choc Lit family for their unerring support. And thanks, as always, to my own family and friends. I love you all.

1

NESSA

I have to tell you that my name is Nessa. *O-ho!* I hear you cry. *That's short for Vanessa, then.*

Well yes. Yes, it is. But I am not called Vanessa.

I am called Agnes.

Which I hate.

But Agnes was my great-great-grandmother's name, you see, and twenty-five years ago, I graced the family by being the first girl born into it in practically a century — so I got the name.

Then I discovered Agnes was a witch's name, so that made it all quite interesting.

And yes, I am currently jumping around the sixteen square metres of my 'garden' and talking to trees, but there's really nothing sinister in it. I'm trying to make a wand, and you have to ask the tree's permission to do that or they get upset. And it's almost Halloween and it's a full moon, so I can't think of a better time to be doing it.

But maybe I should give you a little background? It's all to do with the women in the coffee shop. It's their fault and if it wasn't for them, I wouldn't be doing this.

I suppose at least I'm not jumping around naked though. That's just too much for suburbia to cope with.

EWAN

'Nessa?' I'm rather intrigued as to what my neighbour is doing. She's flouncing around, waving her arms in the air and there's an ominous droning sound coming from her garden.

The last time I heard that noise, I discovered she was actually singing. Maybe she's singing again. If that's the

2

case, I have to stop her before my ears begin to bleed.

'Nessa!' I raise my voice and she stops mid-flounce and looks up at my window. We live in the same building. It's a converted Georgian terrace house, which is now split into flats — she's downstairs, so she gets most of the back garden. I'm upstairs, so I get the little bit in the shade that's tagged onto it. 'Do you need help? Are you in pain? Shall I call an ambulance?'

'Shut up, Ewan Grainger,' she yells back. 'And stop spying on me.'

'I'm not spying on you,' I tell her. 'I'm just concerned for your welfare. You may be having a breakdown of some sort and I want to help you.'

'I am *not*,' she says, 'I'm just — '

But I never find out what Nessa's doing.

'What's *she* doing?' asks Fern, my girlfriend. Her long blonde hair tickles my cheek as she squeezes next to the window beside me and stares down at Nessa.

'I don't know. That's what I'm trying to find out.'

'Well, forget her.' Fern pulls me away from the window and slams it shut. It's an old house and an old window and I'm quite surprised the frame doesn't break. '*I'm* here, and I'd prefer if you focused on *me* rather than your weird neighbour,' she grumbles.

Fern is quite pleasant to look at, with her long blonde hair and her navy-blue eyes. But I don't know — she's not really holding my attention too much tonight. I'm more curious about why Nessa is dancing around the garden during a full moon.

Nessa's a bit strange sometimes, but she's very interesting.

2

NESSA

Ewan has just disappeared from sight, pulled back into the flat like he was sucked into a giant vacuum cleaner. That'll be Fern's doing.

I'm no big fan of Fern. In fact, I think Fern is her own biggest fan. And if I was truly a witch, I'd think up a really good spell just to take her down a peg or two. I pause in my ceremony-thing to think about what I could do to Fern. I come to the conclusion that I'd love to do something about her hair. It's far too sleek and shiny, nothing like my jet-black frizz. But I'm not that bad — horrendous as Fern is, I don't think I would be horrid enough to make her go bald. Maybe she could just have a tragic hair dyeing accident so that the bleach (it's not her natural hair colour, even I can tell that) goes temporarily green.

I turn away from the house and look back at the tree. It's apparently bad luck to cut the branch off the tree to make your wand, so I need to make sure one has fallen off naturally.

And if one hasn't, I am hoping that my leaping around might cause a minor earth tremor and a branch might drop off.

Crack!

Meeeeeeow!

Or I could simply hope my massively fat cat decided to climb the tree.

'Thank you, Schubert!' I shout up at him. 'Remind me to give you extra tuna tomorrow.'

Having said that, I think maybe an excess of tuna has contributed to Schubert's branch-snapping skills. Hmmm. It's a definite possibility.

Anyway, who am I to challenge the laws of the universe? As far as I'm concerned, this branch is going to make a marvellous wand. I just need to consecrate it over my altar first.

I did tell you earlier that I probably needed to give you some background detail, and I realise I should probably do this now before you think I'm just crazy.

Like I said, it's all to do with the coffee shop.

I go there every morning before work. I'm the PA for a private detective, which sounds as if it should be quite interesting and glamorous, but we don't get any massively exciting cases through our doors.

Having said that, we did get a little bit of excitement last month when a batty old lady came in and started insisting her neighbour was trying to steal her shih-poo.

I have to admit I did mishear her at first and didn't quite know how to introduce her to my boss, Mr Hogarth, but it turned out she was talking about her puppy. The puppy was a cross between a shih tzu and a poodle and about the size of a jar of coffee. The shih-poo was very adept at wriggling through the fence. The neighbour was completely innocent and not encouraging it at all, but the lady went to the papers about our 'incompetency' and 'reluctance' in dealing with the situation anyway; Mr Hogarth's initial response was to simply tell her to wait a few weeks until the dog had grown too big to wriggle through the gap.

We had a day of being the 'Shi*-Poor-Agency' (our local newspaper has no imagination) but then it's chip paper anyway. Of course, Ewan saw the headline and had to ask me about it, especially as some dozy reporter must have been camped outside the office all afternoon in order to take that picture of me.

Seriously, I hate having my photo taken on a good day, let alone a day when I'm craving chocolate and have taken the opportunity to stuff a family-size bar of the stuff in my mouth as I'm walking out of the office.

So naturally, the picture that goes in

the paper is of me, wearing a hunted expression and generally looking like a pig. And yes, I'll admit, I was looking furtive. So the picture matched the sleazy, couldn't-care-less-about-old-people-and-puppies image the rag was after.

'That was a classy photo, Nessa,' said Ewan as I bumped into him in the stairwell that evening. He had the paper rolled up like a tube, with my face glaring out of it.

'Get lost, Ewan.' I tried to push past him.

'Now, now. I might have to run my own story about how I live above you and how rude you are.' He was smirking at this point.

'Go away,' I growled and managed to get past him.

His laughter annoyed the hell out of me as I stomped off towards my front door, but I ignored him and slammed my door shut as he stood in the stairwell.

Sometimes I hate my neighbour.

But most of the time I simply fancy

the pants off him.

I found that picture blown up and stuck to my front door a few days later, but annoying as Ewan can be, I know he wouldn't have done that to me. I ripped the thing off, noticing with some disgust that it had been graffiti-ed over with some nasty phrases likening me to a pig, and a snout and trotters had been added in thick, black marker pen. I have an idea of who put it there, but I don't like to say. Not yet.

But I still haven't told you about the coffee shop, have I?

Well it's like this.

Every morning when I go into the coffee shop, there are a group of four women who are always there at the same time as me. The problem I have is that they like the same seats I do.

By taking my window seat, they have, indeed, marked their cards.

I christened them the Coven as they are like a bunch of cackling old witches, and what made this even more appropriate was the book that I found

10

in the coffee shop around that time. This particular day, another lady was sitting in the opposite corner reading. She fussed around so much as she was preparing to leave that she ended up leaving her book behind.

Now this is sacrilege of the worst kind, as you never leave a book behind.

So I jumped out of my seat and scurried over to grab it and return it to her, but by the time I'd picked it up and dashed out of the coffee shop, down the stairs and then out of the front doors, the lady was gone. I stood on the shallow steps staring around me but she must have melted into the crowd by then. She had long, wavy hair, which was the deep, reddish colour of shiny cherry-wood so she should have stuck out a mile, but I couldn't see her at all.

I looked down at the book and saw it was a book on Wicca and witchcraft.

I won't pretend that my heart didn't beat a little faster, and the word 'serendipity' sprang into my mind

— which is just a literary way of saying 'oh my, what a wonderful coincidence' — and I found myself turning the book over in my hands and thinking.

And then I thought that I might as well keep it and read it myself.

And then it got me thinking about witches and witchiness in general, and yes, that old great-great-grandmother of mine.

I wondered if she had been a witch, because there were a few strange stories about her, handed down the generations: The rumour was that she used love potions like 'other people use toilet water'. But I suspect that particular rumour might have been started by some jealous ladies who didn't like all the male attention she was getting.

Aggie was supposed to be drop-dead gorgeous; the original wild-child and some sort of courtesan to King Edward VII. But having said that, most beautiful women were courtesans of that fine King, so you can't be too sure.

My father has a photograph of her,

which shows her in full court regalia — not that we believe she had any right to court regalia — and she has the same sort of hair as me, which is dark and curly and pretty untameable. It's one of those pictures that's been hand coloured, and whoever did it gave her bright green eyes, so she looks a bit like a cat. She also looks like she's going to burst out laughing.

Nobody knew who my great-grandfather's father was — for sure, Aggie never married and there is no name on the birth certificate, but as her lifestyle was rather grand and she had a huge house in the borders, a lovely town house in Edinburgh New Town and a *pied á terre* in London, I don't think Aggie missed out on having a man in her life. Or, shall we say, one *particular* man. I believe she had quite a few *men*. One of them probably paid for the houses she lived in.

My parents still live in the Edinburgh house — we were all brought up there, all five of us: Billy, Scott, Hugo, Alfie and me. It was a very noisy house and I spent much of my childhood covered in mud and spiders — but it never did me any harm.

I suspect that my parents were slightly shocked when I made my appearance — nobody quite knew what to do with me, except curse me hideously with that dreadful name. I do know that Scott used to like to put ribbons in my hair and change my clothes quite regularly, as if I was a giant doll — he's always had an eye for co-ordination which makes him an awesome designer nowadays. The rest of my brothers used to largely hit me. But that's okay, because I'd hit them back and I'd still hit them back now if I had to; but I'd also turn on anyone who hurt *them* and I damn well know how to stand up for myself, so I have much to be grateful for. Apart from my name, of course, but I can't help that.

But I digress.

A few years earlier, I think poor Agnes would have been burnt at the stake, simply for being pretty and popular and suspected of the Dark Arts, but in the early 1900s she was quite safe.

That's very good to know, because I think I'll be quite safe when I look into it a bit further and —

'Oh, very classy, young lady,' I mutter.

Fern has just stuck her own head out of Ewan's window and given me a V-sign, before closing the curtains again. I give a V-sign back to the window. Fern is definitely going to be my test subject. I've decided.

And then I look around the garden, and I suddenly wonder where my cat is.

3

EWAN

'What was the point of that?' I ask Fern. I just saw what she did to Nessa, but she mustn't have known I was watching — I'd left the room to get a bottle of wine and some glasses out of the kitchen. Fern blushes.

'She deserved it. She keeps staring up here.'

'Probably because she's worried someone's spying on her.'

Fern flicks that hair back over her shoulder and sniffs tetchily. 'I just don't like her, okay? The sooner you move out of here and in with me, the better.'

'I'm not moving anywhere, any time soon,' I say to Fern.

I'm a bit sick of this discussion, to be honest. She brings it up far too frequently for my liking. She won't let things happen naturally. As it is, she's always round here, and it gets a bit too much at times.

'I'm always round here, anyway,' she says.

See what I mean?

'But you can go home and we can both enjoy our own space at the minute,' I tell her, pouring the wine.

'There's not much wine in that bottle is there?' Fern says, pulling a face. I knew the wine would distract her. She likes her wine, does Fern.

'No,' I reply. 'It's what I had left from yesterday.' I don't bother telling her I have two more full bottles hidden away.

I can't really tell her that a fuller bottle will encourage her to stay longer and I've suddenly gone off the idea of spending a lot of time with her tonight.

I met Fern at a club in London about a year ago, when I was DJ-ing — there we were, both a bit worse for wear, miles away from our native Edinburgh, and we clicked in a melee of sweaty bodies and alcohol. It was a lot of fun and she was really interested in what I was doing — she said she'd heard of me, which made me feel brilliant. I wrote a massively successful novel about organised crime in the club scene, you see, and there was talk from my agent about selling the film rights. That finally happened about six months ago, and Fern's excited to think that she'll meet Vinnie Jones and Jude Law when they film it down in Chelsea next year.

It can still be fun with Fern, but sometimes part of me wonders if it's me she wants, or the status of being with Ewan Grainger the Famous Author. Or perhaps she prefers the abandoned joy of dancing and gyrating up on the podium with Ewan G, the slightly wild and now notable, in-demand DJ?

I know it's a bizarre mixture — nobody ever said I was an easy person to pigeonhole — but to be honest I'm trying to put the club-land stuff behind me now, despite it paying very well. I want to concentrate more on the writing.

At the minute, the celebrity magazines can't get enough of my weirdly diverse passions — but to me, it's just creativity coming out in a different way, be it via music or words. Honestly, the media are making such a fuss over that film, but Fern's been great about fielding the questions and working the PR. She's in marketing anyway, so knows a thing or two about how to handle it, and she's enjoyed the attention a lot more than I have.

I'm basically just trying to get to grips with writing the screenplay and working out the soundtrack — and I'm going to cameo as a DJ, apparently, and it's such a lot of hard work. Maybe I'm just not paying her enough attention, and the guilt I feel over that is making me want to get shot of her tonight.

But despite all that, I don't like the way she's always so mean to Nessa. It's not funny. Nessa is the only person she seems to have a problem with, which I find quite peculiar. I like Nessa. I like Nessa very much and she doesn't deserve the barbed comments at all.

'Oh. Sorry, I meant to tell you, I have an early start tomorrow,' I suddenly say, in, I feel, an inspired fashion, 'so would you mind going home tonight?' I give her what I hope is a winning smile.

'But it's Saturday tomorrow!'

'Yeah.' It's my turn to pull a face. 'But I have to go away early. I've got a research trip. I've got to meet someone about something and it's over in Perthshire.'

'Perthshire?' she says, in surprise. I suspect she's trying to think of which clubs I'll be working in, in Perthshire. 'Well, I wouldn't mind going there. I've heard there are some — um — nice shops there. Yes. Some nice shops.'

'Perth*shire*,' I say. 'Not *Perth*. Not the town.'

Ferns stares at me blankly. 'But I like shops.'

'I know, sweetheart.' I glug the last of the wine into her glass, simply to use it up. 'But we both live in Edinburgh. We have good shops here.'

'You're an author. You don't have to leave the house to meet people,' says Fern, trying a different tactic. I have half an eye on her glass and half an eye on the window. I want to pull back those curtains again and see what Nessa is up to; there's some God-awful caterwauling going on and I'm not sure if it's her or Schubert.

'There's no substitute for speaking to people,' I say, slightly distracted by thoughts of Nessa dancing around the garden. In my thoughts, she is naked.

Fern drains her glass and looks at it in some surprise. 'Oh. It's empty.'

'What a shame,' I say. 'Here, let me call you a taxi. It's late and I've had wine too so I can't drive you home.'

Fern blinks at me. 'Are you trying to get rid of me?' she asks accusingly.

'Of course not,' I lie.

'Because if it's *her* . . . '

'It's nobody. It's nothing except that

I have to be up early!' I tell her. Smoothly, I hand her a cardigan, or a shrug, or whatever they're called.

She takes it, but I'm not sure if she believes my story. It was a rather ingenious story though. And there *is* something I want to look at in Perthshire. But it isn't going to run away. And it does seem a lot more appealing to head to Perthshire and not live in my head, in a dingy London club, for another weekend, trying to put words into Vinnie's mouth.

NESSA

I can hear Schubert making that horrendous noise he's so fond of when he's out trying to impress the lady-cats. Poor sod, he's never going to get a girlfriend with that noise coming out of his mouth.

I think he's on next door's roof. If you can imagine the scene in *Mary Poppins* when Dick van Dyke is singing about chimney sweeps, then that's what the roofline of our terrace looks like. We have a ton of old chimneys and nooks and crannies galore — because the houses used to be big old three-storey mansions and they aren't any more but nobody told the chimneys that.

From Ewan's flat, you can actually climb out of the attic window and onto the roof. I have done this on a few occasions when Schubert has got stuck. I can always tell when he's stuck because he stops singing and starts whimpering instead. Bloody stupid animal that he is; I mean Schubert, not Ewan, of course.

Ewan uses part of the top floor as his workspace. He writes books, and he's rather famous now, but I've never read any of his books. I think he likes to concentrate on detective novels or crime stories because he used to be in the special branch or something until he made it big. Mr Hogarth, my boss, speaks very highly of Ewan and his family. Ewan's dad was in the business as was his granddad and blah blah blah and so on through the generations. And as Mr Hogarth is Ewan's godfather, of course he's going to be proud of him. Mr Hogarth is also our landlord, but we don't use the word 'nepotism' at all around here; however, it's very handy if I'm late with my rent, which has happened on one or two occasions. But still, I bet one of Ewan's relatives would have put Aggie on trial if she'd been around in the 1600s.

The rest of Ewan's extra floor is storage, divided up by a soundproof door, because he DJs as well and he's got turntables or mixers or a recording studio or whatever it is in there. The soundproofing obviously works because he doesn't make a great deal of noise with his music.

I sort of wish I had the basement flat for my workspace. I don't actually have a need for a workspace, but it would be nice to have it, wouldn't it?

But a young couple live in the basement flat and they seem to be in a perpetual haze of marijuana. They're very friendly, but I don't think they always know who they're talking to. They're a bit like hippies, I suppose and she always wears a kaftan thing. We smile and nod, and they travel to a lot of festivals. I know this because they have a tiny pop up tent and they use the paved area in front of their flat to dry the tent out after Glastonbury and the like. It can stay there for days until they drift out and realise it's probably become wetter with the Scottish rain than it had been when they put it there.

At least the rain washes the mud off.

Oh, and it stinks inside the tent. I know this, because last week I had to get Schubert out of there after a bad-boy torn cat chased him in and I could hear him crying. Schubert has a distinctive cry — cat-like yet pathetic. Pizza usually cheers him up no end, and sometimes I wonder if he just does the crying thing to make me feel sorry for him.

EWAN

The caterwauling is still going on, and it's turned into that whimpering sound Schubert makes when he realises how high up he is. It's coming from right outside my window.

The taxi's arrived, anyway, so I shove Fern out of the door with a swift goodnight kiss and I hurry up to the top floor to peer out of the window, and sure enough, there's Schubert, hanging onto a chimney pot with his eyes actually closed — his vocal gymnastics are wretched in the extreme.

Well, I could easily climb out of the window myself, but it's so much more fun to knock on the floor and get Nessa up. Plus, Schubert refuses to come to me when he's in a mood like that. He just wants his mum.

There's a set of stairs in her flat that lead up to mine, which are left over from when the flats were a house. Nessa uses them as a bookcase and a house-plant stand. Sometimes I think it would be a good idea to cut a trapdoor in the floor so I can just open it up and let Nessa in that way for Mission Schubert, but I don't think she'd be too impressed. And Fern would probably tip boiling oil down it anyway.

So I grab the mop, go downstairs and bash on the floor three times, which is the Schubert Signal. I go to my front door and open it again, and then I hear Nessa's front door slam below me.

I see a dark figure heading up the staircase, then there's a flash of light and lots of swearing.

4

NESSA

I just can't believe it. I was heading out to Ewan's flat, summoned by the Schubert Signal, when some idiot leaped out of the shadows, stuck a camera in my face and took a flash photograph.

When I can see clearly again and without a white light searing my vision, I recognise the idiot reporter from the local paper who was responsible for the Chocolate Shot.

'What the bloody hell do you think you're doing?' I shriek. 'I'll have you arrested!' Too late, I realise I'm still holding my wand and brandishing it at him. 'That's illegal!'

'I'm acting on a tip off,' says the reporter. He's a horribly oily sort of chap with a permanent sheen to his lips where he keeps licking them and greasy hair plastered to the sides of his face *á la* Shane MacGowan on a particularly bad day. 'And that's assault with a deadly weapon.' He nods at my wand and smirks at me.

'It's a tree branch!' I say and brandish it again. Which is maybe not the best thing to say or do under the circumstances.

'It's a kosh,' he says.

'It's self-defence,' I fire back.

Ewan appears at the top of the staircase with his arms folded and stares down at us. I half expect him to do the well-worn policeman routine and go, 'What's all this then?'

But he doesn't.

'Can I help?' he asks smoothly. 'Or shall I call the police and tell them we have an intruder on the property?'

'I'm acting on a tip-off,' repeats the reporter. 'I was told there were drugs on the premises. Specifically,' he looks at me, 'on the first-floor landing.'

'Drugs?' Ewan and I say together.

Then I go hot and cold as I recall the small plastic bag of suspect plant matter Schubert kindly brought to my front door after the tent incident downstairs. I assume he thought he was rewarding me for rescuing him from Monster Cat. I dropped it casually back down into their yard on the way to work but somebody must have seen Schubert with it, and *I've* had no visitors so —

'Cowbag,' I mutter.

Fern is such a bitch.

'I assure you,' says Ewan, advancing down a few stairs and coming to stand next to me, 'there are no drugs on this property.'

I can see the reporter shrinking a little against the wall. Ewan has to be six foot three and he used to play rugby at university — so you can imagine his general size. There's not an ounce of fat on him mind, he's solid muscle and next to Mr Licky Lips Stick Man Ewan Grainger, with his short dark brown hair and his steely grey eyes, is rather imposing.

I try not to think about the small yet sexy tattoo on Ewan's shoulder blade and how the muscles had rippled under it when I'd spotted him digging up weeds, in his scrap of garden, in the summer. Instead, I try to concentrate on the matter at hand.

I feel a bit braver now Ewan is there and I've stopped going hot and cold, so I move forwards as well and scowl at Sticky. 'Who told you that?' I ask, 'because I'll have them arrested as well.'

'That's classified,' says Sticky and I roll my eyes. I hate that expression — it makes me think of people plucking out their eyeballs and playing marbles with them; but I did actually roll my eyes heavenwards before letting them settle on Sticky again.

'Classified?' I say. Then I roll my eyes again for good effect. 'I bet you've been desperate to say that for years. Have you been practising? 'Oooh, look at me, I'm a fake paparazzo and it is all classified . . . '' I start mincing around, imitating what I think Sticky would do and Ewan reaches out a hand and puts it firmly on my shoulder. He makes his point and I stop mincing before we lose the battle.

'All right,' says Ewan, ever so calmly and ever so deadly, 'I won't make you talk this time, but I strongly suggest you get your facts right before trespassing on private property again.'

Sticky nods briefly and turns around. He scurries down the stairs and then I hear him scurry out of the building and away into the night like the rat he is.

I am so very angry at Fern I think I'm just about to explode. I wish Sticky would start stalking *her* instead, and then we could see how *she* liked it.

But once we're sure the reporter has gone, I turn to Ewan and brandish my wand at him.

'You tell your stupid girlfriend to get her facts right before she tries to mess up my life again, okay? I'm just about sick of her and her accusations. It's not the first time, you know, and I don't know what I've ever done to her. I swear that she's the one who stuck that horrible paparazzi picture to our front door.'

Ewan looks at me in some surprise, then it's like a shutter comes down over his face. Bugger, I've just dissed his girlfriend to his face. Hey ho. And I have no proof, do I? Whoops.

'You want to come and get your cat?' Ewan asks me.

His voice is toneless and he turns away from me. He takes the stairs two at a time and disappears around the dog-leg to his floor. Maybe this is just what happens when you're a famous author-type person. Maybe the paparazzi just come and creep around outside your house to act on tip-offs, trying to get a good story. Maybe Fern would appear as the victim or something in the article, looking all sad and pathetic and going, 'Oh, oh, oh, my boyfriend lives near a drug baron, oh, oh, oh, I'm so worried for his life.'

I trail up after him and walk into his flat. He's left the door open, but he hasn't waited for me.

Bugger.

EWAN

I really can't believe what Nessa has just told me. Well, I can, given the way Fern's been behaving towards her recently. Would it be better to say I don't *want* to believe it?

I think it's a good job Fern has gone home. The last thing I want is a war on the staircase. One nutter pap-hack is enough for tonight. Just out of curiosity, though, I think I'll check the drawer beside my bed. I took the photo of Nessa out of the paper and tucked it in there. I have no idea why. It wasn't the most flattering of shots, but it was kind of cute and funny and cheered me up to see it.

'Can I just climb out the window, then?' asks Nessa. She's in the hallway shuffling from foot to foot and looking a bit awkward.

I smile at her, distracted, and nod. 'Yeah. You know the drill.' I turn my attention back to my bedroom.

'Okay,' she says. Then there's her footsteps on the narrow staircase, and the sound of the window opening.

But I can't resist. I pop my head out of the bedroom just long enough to see her reach the top of the stairs and begin to climb out of the window. That damned stick is lying on the hallway floor and I still have no idea what she's doing with it anyway.

'Ewan Grainger', she says, her voice kind of muffled because she's half in and half out of the window. 'Are you looking at my bum?'

'No,' I lie, and duck back into the bedroom.

I open up the drawer and move a few socks around. I move a few more socks around. There's nothing in there except socks. I open up the other drawers and they are all in order as well. Nothing out of place.

There's no newspaper photo anywhere to be seen.

5

NESSA

Schubert is being particularly obnoxious and silly. He's got his eyes closed and he's mewing pitifully. It would be quite comical if he wasn't my cat and I didn't have to witness him clenching his claws around a chimney pot with his fur all stuck up on end. He looks like a crazy animal, silhouetted against the giant full moon, yet illuminated by the landing light.

'Come on,' I coax. 'Tuna time.' I swear he shakes his head and squeezes his eyes shut even more. His meow sounds like a 'Nooooooooooo!' covering a good three octaves.

I ease myself towards him, because any sharp actions will make him bolt, even though he appears too terrified to move. He shuffles around the chimney pot away from me and cries. Good grief.

'Schubert. Come on. Come to mummy.'

He makes a subdued sniffing noise and half opens one eye. I can see his fur start to relax and I know we've almost won. 'Catnip wants to see you,' I say and bring a bedraggled mouse thing out of my pocket. The trick with Schubert is to get his attention then produce Catnip. Schubert has loved Catnip the Mouse since he was a kitten and slept with him every night. Catnip has his own blanket and Schubert noses him underneath it and pats the blanket down around him.

'Good boy,' I say and wave Catnip around a bit, hoping the scent will reach Schubert. I'm not disappointed.

Schubert opens his eyes fully and fixes his gaze on Catnip. He meows querulously once or twice, then unwinds a paw which he stretches out to me. I back slowly away and sure enough, Schubert disconnects himself from the chimney pot and stalks towards me, watching Catnip all the time.

The awkward bit is the window. I have discovered that the best thing to do is to throw Catnip through it. Schubert leaps in after him and then I climb in, shutting it firmly behind me.

This is what we do today and I head back down to the main floor and stand in the hallway and watch as Schubert ecstatically rolls around with his toy. Ewan usually stands down there waiting for me. He gives me a round of applause and Schubert a cat threat; but I notice with some regret that Ewan isn't doing that tonight and the hallway is empty.

It was that Fern thing, wasn't it?

All I can say, is *Shi*-Poor*.

EWAN

From the noise in the hallway, I can guess that Schubert has been rescued.

I've missed my chance at applause, thanks to my preoccupation with Fern.

'I'll be going now!' calls Nessa in an odd flat little voice. 'Come on Schubert, come here.' The sounds of ecstatic cat-ness stop and I guess she's picked the beast up now and is currently staggering to the door under the weight.

'Nessa, wait!' I call and hurry into the hallway. I'm right. The apparition that turns to greet me is a fat cat on two legs.

'Ewan,' she replies and looks at me. Well, I assume she's looking at me. Her feet are pointed in my direction, as is Schubert. I can't see her face due to the cat.

And before I can think, the words are out.

'I've just opened a bottle of wine. Fancy a drink?'

There is the briefest pause, then a curious sounding 'Okay', from behind the cat's right ear.

She bends down and puts the animal

on the floor, where it recommences ecstatic Catnip-play. Schubert loves that mouse.

'Great!' I say. 'Oh, and don't forget your stick.'

It startles me slightly when she says, quite matter-of-factly, 'Oh it's not a stick, it's a wand.'

NESSA

There now, it's out. I've told him about my wand and he probably thinks I am as much of a nutter as the reporter.

'A wand?' he says. He takes a couple of steps towards me and I kind of shrink back.

'Uh-huh. Um. No. No, it's not. It's not really a wand. It's a wand-like stick. It's . . . it's Schubert's,' I say ingeniously. Schubert, hearing his name, looks at me, then goes back to Catnip. He completely ignores the stick. 'See,' I say, 'he loves it. Can't keep him away from it.'

'A wand,' Ewan repeats. He folds his arms and sort of looms over me. I feel a little like that reporter must have done. I pull myself up to my full height of five foot four and fold my arms too. God, Ewan is tall close up.

'A stick,' I say. But I can feel my cheeks burning.

He's not only tall he's dangerously gorgeous and I feel a little short of breath next to him.

Oh my.

'No it's *not* a stick, Nessa. We both know it's a wand,' he says. 'Well now, that's rather good. Come on. Come with me before this wine evaporates and I shall tell you why it's a good thing.' Then he grins at me and turns around. I scurry after him, with a quick look back at Schubert to make sure he's okay.

Once we are seated in Ewan's lounge, he pours me a large glass of red and smiles at me. 'So tell me, Nessa. What do you want a wand for? Are you interested in witches?'

I laugh, a little self-consciously, and shrug my shoulders. 'I suppose so. There's a rumour that my great-great-grandmother was one, but I don't think it's true. I'm named after her. She was a courtesan of King Edward and a bit of a tart, I think. She was pretty popular with the men and we don't know anything about my great-grandfather's paternity, but she seemed to do all right out of it.

'I'm just named after her, though, you understand. I'm not a bit like her. I'm not a courtesan or anything. I haven't got any children out of wedlock and I'm rarely in the gossip pages, unless you count that article,' I say, rather hurriedly.

I don't know why I'm volunteering this information; maybe it's something to do with the fact that the wine is very relaxing and Ewan's lounge is nice and warm. After all, it's the end of October and it's dark if you don't count the moonlight and it's not the most pleasant of temperatures to be outside doing a Dick van Dyke, is it?

'Oh!' he says and leans closer to me. So close, in fact, that I can smell his aftershave and it's a nice one. It smells a bit like Christmas trees. 'So she was called Vanessa too? It's a pretty name.'

'Agnes,' I say before I can stop myself. Ugh. There I go again; there's no need for him to hear that. It's nothing I've ever, ever, shared with him before. But give him his due, there is only the briefest flicker of distaste on his face as the fact I am called 'Agnes' sinks in. I blink and look at him, wondering what his next comment will be.

'Agnes,' he says slowly. 'That's pretty too. I suppose.' Then the corner of his mouth twitches into the beginning of a smile. 'Actually — ' he begins; then he smiles properly and shakes his head.

'We both know that it's not a pretty name!' I say, laughing. 'It's an awful name. I'm cursed with that name. But I'm the only girl, see, and so I got it.'

'I see,' he says, nodding. He reaches

for the bottle of wine and tops my glass up. A little bit sloshes over the side and I raise the glass to my mouth and lick the drops off. I'm conscious that he's watching me and it makes me blush a little more.

'I'm just wondering,' says Ewan, 'if you'd be interested in a proposition?'

I sit up straight and blink. A proposition? Does he mean what I think he means?

'But what about Fern?' I blurt out.

Ewan looks at me oddly. 'I don't think Fern would be interested, to be honest, and I think you would be.' He leans closer. 'You see, I need someone and — '

'Yes!' I practically shout. Maybe he wants me to strip here and now and get naked or jiggy with it. God, I've surprised *myself* by even agreeing to it so quickly. It's the wine, it has to be, because —

'But you don't even know what I want yet!' he says. He sits back and stares at me.

'It's fine, really, whatever you want,' I say and smile at him. Oooh six foot three of rugby player and those eyes . . .

'You'd want to traipse to Perthshire with me and look at an ancient monument?'

'I . . . what?'

'Ancient monument. In Perthshire. You really want to visit it?' He smiles at me again and looks so grateful I can't even answer just at this moment. My mouth opens and closes like a fish's and I feel myself nodding out of sheer embarrassment.

God, I'm glad I kept my clothes on.

'Well. Yes. Ancient monuments,' I manage eventually. I force a smile onto my face, feeling my lips stretching in a fake sort of fashion and knowing I probably look more like a sinister vampire than a person who is really, really excited about going to see an ancient monument. In Perthshire. For goodness sake.

'I love ancient monuments,' I say in a small voice. 'I really do.'

How quickly can I get out of this place? I eye the space on the floor where I am pretty certain my staircase-that's-not-a-staircase would end up and I wonder if the combined weight of me and Schubert leaping on it would break through the floor and I could drop into my own flat as quickly as possible.

Then with any luck I might break my neck and die and I wouldn't have to think about this ever again.

'Well,' says Ewan, 'it might not *be* an ancient monument.' He leans over the side of his chair and gropes around for something. I quickly knock back the rest of my wine.

He pops back up, holding a book in his hand. Then his eyes widen as he sees my empty glass. 'You want some more? I've got plenty.'

I shake my head, regretting swigging it back as it almost choked me and it's difficult to choke quietly in someone's lounge.

'Oh, well if you're sure,' he says and hands over the book. 'This book is about the ancient monument I mentioned. It's a monument to Maggie Wall, a woman burnt as a witch in 1657.'

'Oh!' I say, intrigued despite myself. I grab the book from him and flick through it eagerly. It's called *Maggie Wall-The Witch Who Never Was* and it's by a chap called Geoff Holder.

'Yes, Geoff, the author,' says Ewan, as if he knows this guy personally, 'did a fair amount of research on it. He suggests that it's a fake. Evidence suggests that it was a folly built in the eighteenth century and there never was a witch called Maggie Wall. It's really interesting. She never appears in any paperwork and there are no official records of her even existing.'

I chance a quick look at Ewan and his eyes are sparkling.

'I'm sick of club-land screenplays and want a break. I want a fresh start and a new book to play with and this is the best opportunity I've had in ages. I've decided my latest crime novel is going to be set in the area and I want to do some research.'

'Did a witch do the crime?' I ask and Ewan shrugs.

'I don't know,' he says simply, 'the book will tell me when I write it.'

I think that's a bit weird for an author to say that, but I don't know much about writing books so I let it go.

'Geoff's book looks like a good book,' I say. 'When are you going?'

'Well,' says Ewan,' is tomorrow too short notice for you?'

I think of the million and one things I need to do this weekend and there can be only one answer.

'Not at all,' I say, 'so long as Schubert can come along.'

6

EWAN

This morning isn't exactly going as planned. I don't know what possessed me to invite Nessa along, but it seemed like — and still does seem like — a good idea. I'm just a little concerned about how we transport a fat, nervous cat for one hour or so through Scotland.

Nessa says she has a cat basket that he likes, and so long as he has Catnip he should be all right.

So far, so good. But the issue I'm having at the minute is that my car won't start. This is not a good thing.

'Is everything okay?' Nessa has appeared beside me, with a pink cat transporter and Schubert sitting inside it like a Sphinx, one paw placed carefully over Catnip. Nessa looks really nice this morning, dressed for the weather in a chunky sweater, faded jeans, knee length boots and a red scarf that sets off her hair.

'Not really,' I admit, coming out from under the bonnet of my car. 'It's just not starting. I don't know what it is.'

'Starting motor? Cam belt? Carburettor issues? Flat battery?'

I look at Nessa with a new kind of respect. 'All of them? None of them?' I say, and shrug my shoulders. 'Sorry, I don't know just yet. I can probably find out, but it'll take a while and I see His Lordship is ready for the off. I'm sorry.'

Nessa comes and stands next to me and peers into the engine. 'Yes. I could probably find out as well, but you're right, it will take a while.'

'What?' I ask stupidly.

'I have four brothers. I know a bit about engines. They're very boring — engines are boring, that is, not my brothers, but my brothers also have their moments. Let's just take Winnie.'

'Winnie?' I ask, even more stupidly. Then I get a nervous feeling in the pit of my stomach. 'You mean — take *that* thing?' I nod over to Nessa's parking space.

Winnie is a small, yellow camper van. It has swathes of green and blue flowers painted all over it and I remember watching, fascinated, as Nessa repainted all the flowers last spring. Her tongue was poking out from between her teeth as she concentrated and she looked really sweet.

'Yes. Winnie Bago,' she says and smiles. 'She's quite safe since Hugo sorted out the brakes and we realised the air intake pipe was in the wrong way.' She shakes her head as if remembering something unpleasant. 'That's why she was sucking through the fuel. Yes. So, we'll go in Winnie, eh?' She stares at me, a challenge in her eyes. I look down at Schubert and he's staring at me the same way. Without taking his eyes off me, he scoops Catnip towards him and hisses quietly. He's not going to let me say no, is he?

'Schubert's been looking forward to the trip,' says Nessa, as if validating the animal. 'Do you *really* want to let him down? We discussed it all last night and he's very excited.'

I'm a wee bit nervous now. Refuse to travel in the sardine tin and risk the wrath of my downstairs neighbours (both human and feline), or travel in the thing and take my life in my hands. What a decision.

'We go in Winnie,' I hear myself say.

Nessa beams and it's like the sun has come out.

'Great!' she says. 'Just watch Schubert a second and I'll get the keys.'

She plonks the carrier on the ground and Schubert watches her go. Then he turns to me and purrs loudly.

Maybe he's not too bad a cat, I think.

I also think, I hope my life insurance is up to date and my Will is easily accessible, in case anything happens to me during my time in Winnie.

NESSA

I really don't know why Ewan looked so nervous when we started driving. Winnie spluttered a little, but that's fair enough; she hasn't had a good long run since the summer.

I just fancied taking her up to Dunning today — the village in Perthshire that Ewan wants to visit. Winnie's not done too badly so far, apart from that weird smell of burning when we were stuck in the traffic.

And I even swept a few things off the dashboard to show Ewan Winnie's tape-deck. It, like Winnie, is vintage, but it's only snarled up a couple of tapes, and they weren't very good ones anyway. 'Look. You can put one of your dancey dancey beat tape things on if you want,' I tell Ewan. I jiggle my shoulders a little and smile at him, to show I'd be very happy to listen to some dancey dancey beat music if he wished to put it on. I quite like listening to music in Winnie, but I prefer to keep the volume low so I can hear if any bits drop off her.

'I . . . I don't think I've played a tape in about fifteen years,' he says in a funny, wooden-type voice. His eyes are fixed firmly on the road ahead and his hands are clutching the seat so his knuckles gleam white through his skin.

'What's wrong?' I ask kindly.

'I wish you'd keep your eyes on the road. Didn't you hear that lorry tooting?'

'Oh,' I say blithely, 'people are always tooting at Winnie. She loves it. Doesn't she, Schubert?'

'Mow wow,' agrees Schubert and I nod.

'We weren't too close to the lorry at *all*, Schubert, you're right,' I tell him.

Nothing fell off Winnie, thankfully, but we gave her a little rest at the service station overlooking the Forth Bridge. I let Schubert out of his basket for a sniff around while we're there. Well, I opened the door and he stuck his nose out, it twitched and he withdrew again, much as a turtle withdraws into its shell. He is a most peculiar cat. You would have thought he would have wanted to explore a little before settling down for the next leg of the journey.

Anyway, as we are sitting in the car park preparing to continue northwards, Ewan begins rustling around with some papers and spreads a map out in front of him. Winnie isn't huge, by any means, but once Ewan and his documents are out, it seems as if there's barely any room for me and Schubert. We squish up on a bench seat, watching Ewan cover all the surfaces with paperwork.

'Maggie Wall,' he mutters. 'It's the name of the fields, you know. Possibly derived from the old name 'Muggie's Wall', which might mean a field full of sheep. Sheep that have been penned in. With walls.'

'Do you *really* think there were witches around at that time?' I ask him, watching him scribble some notes down in a delightfully large and inviting-looking notebook.

'Undoubtedly,' he says. 'They were executed in the woods, just up the road from the town.' He looks at me and his eyes twinkle. 'We could go there as well, if you fancy it. Kincladie Wood. It's not far from the monument, and it might even be haunted.'

'Okay,' I say meeting his eyes steadily. If he thinks I am one of these girly girls who flinch at that sort of story, he's wrong. 'What do I tell Fern if the ghosts get you?'

'Fern?' He looks at me blankly for a moment. 'Oh. Fern. I don't know. Tell her the truth, I guess.' He shrugs his shoulders and looks back at his maps.

'I haven't read any of your books, Ewan,' I tell him. 'I'm sorry about that.'

'That's okay,' he says, his attention not leaving the papers. 'I haven't had to use your investigation company either. There's nobody I want to be tracked and no mysteries that need solving, so there you go.'

'The agency is really very boring,' I say. 'I've been reading a lot about witches, with being related to Aggie, you know, and I've made a kind of altar on my desk at work, just to meditate on because it fascinated me so much. Earth, air, fire and water. A pot plant, a feather, a candle and a bottle of water. It's so quiet at the moment in the agency, I can at least use my time productively by meditating. But don't tell my boss please.'

'That's an odd collection of things, and an even odder way to admit to using them. I think this Aggie thing is getting to you.'

'Maybe,' I say. 'I have to dedicate my wand next. I'm not sure how to do it. I haven't got to that part of the book yet.'

'The book?' He pops his head up and frowns at me.

'Yes, I have a book. I was never born with the knowledge, you know. I have to learn it somehow.'

'Well don't go messing with things you don't understand.'

'That's why I have the book. So I can learn.'

'Hmmm?'

'I found the book in the coffee shop where the Coven lurk,' I tell him. I shift my weight and Winnie shifts with it, creaking a bit.

'The *Coven*?' he practically shouts. His eyes are wide open and I've definitely got his attention now.

'Yes. I think they're witches. They cackle a lot.' Schubert hisses, agreeing with me even though he's never met them.

'Okay. They might *not* be witches, you know,' says Ewan, ever so carefully.

'But they might be,' I reply.

Ewan is silent and blinks. 'Okay. Are you ready to go?'

'Yeah. I'm just waiting for you.'

'Fine.' He folds the papers and the maps up, back along the proper creases and everything. He makes them really neat. I know I would make a mess of them, and I equally know that I wouldn't even try to fold them back up.

That's why Winnie is strewn with maps and leaflets and they're shoved in her drawers any which way.

It's quite nice, in some respects, as it's a good way of me remembering where I've visited. Winnie is quite old but she's equally well travelled, even from just being with me. One year, we did John O'Groats *and* Land's End during the summer — straight along the centre of Britain, with a few diversions here and there as I fancied it. That's the year I met Schubert — a straggly, mangy, kitten hanging around the Norfolk Broads.

The chap at the lock told me that the kitten had probably been thrown off a boat, and the owners hadn't come back for him. Schubert had been soaking wet and half-drowned, and had been discovered huddling by the lock keeper's cottage. When I picked him up, he cuddled into me and we went into the nearest town and bought Catnip there and then. We also bought his blanket and the pink cat transporter as they didn't have any other colours in the place.

Schubert is a lovely cat and those boat people need to be thrown into jail.

EWAN

Nessa has a face like thunder and she's scowling really badly as she settles into the driver's seat and rams Winnie into first gear.

'Why do you have a face like thunder and why are you scowling so much?' I ask her, quickly fastening my seatbelt as we kangaroo-hop out of the car park.

'I'm thinking about Norfolk,' says Nessa and crunches the van into second.

'I like Norfolk,' I say pathetically.

'Oh, me too!' Nessa turns her face towards me. All of a sudden, her expression is open and friendly and pretty again. 'There was just something unpleasant that happened there and I was remembering it.'

I feel myself bristle and have an urge to rip my shirt off and go all Tarzan.

'What happened? Do I need to exact revenge for you?'

Nessa laughs and the sound makes my He-Man instincts dissolve and I laugh with her — although I'm not certain what we're laughing at yet.

'Oh no,' she says. 'I think we're beyond that. Someone dumped Schubert in a canal and that's how I found him. I was just remembering what he looked like when I got him. Poor little thing.'

I cast a sidelong glance at Cat Mountain, who is presently crooning something to Catnip and I make a non-committal noise that sounds something like 'Hrumph.' I try to make it sound a bit like a question, and I think it works as Nessa nods, making her curls bounce up and down off her shoulders.

'Yes, he was so scrawny, bless him. He's much healthier now, though. That's why he's nervous if he gets into a scrape he can't get out of. I think it brings it all back to him.'

I murmur something like, 'Aaaah,' and that seems to relax Nessa even more.

She smiles again and agrees with me. 'I know,' she says. 'Bless him.' This cat is obviously well blessed. Still, he seems content enough and my thoughts return to witches.

'So tell me more about your witchy research,' I say. If I'm smart, she won't know I might use some of her information in my book.

I'm clearly not smart.

'Will you use my information in your book?' she asks and I cough a little to hide my embarrassment.

'Maybe,' I say. 'You'll be famous.'

'I already am,' she says wryly. The gear lever crunches again as she scowls. 'I know she's your girlfriend and everything, but the drug tip-off thing was out of order, Ewan. I just have to say that to clear the air between us.'

'That's perfectly understandable,' I

say, surprised, 'but I didn't think there was anything to clear between us two. I mean, between you and me.'

'Oh that's all right, then,' she says. 'It's just she's the only one who could have said something and I do think she put that first picture up as well. She's not a very nice person, in my opinion.' Then she kind of bites her lip as if she thinks she's said too much.

'She has her redeeming features,' I say weakly. *But you know what — at this present moment in time, I can't think of any.* 'You haven't told me about your research, anyway,' I prompt, hoping to change the subject.

'Well there's not much to tell.' I think she's secretly relieved about the subject change. 'I have an altar, I have a wand. I'm going to dedicate the altar and I might try a simple candle spell to see if it works.'

'Any thoughts as to what candle spell you might try?'

'I don't know. A friend for Schubert. Good news. A windfall.' Then she glances towards me without turning her head and I swear there is mischief there. 'A tragic hair dyeing accident. A broken pair of hair-straighteners. A frazzled hairdryer.' I know she's thinking about Fern and I turn my head to the window so she doesn't see me smile.

'No love potions?' I ask.

'No love potions,' she replies firmly. 'I don't need them.'

'Oh,' I say. And continue looking out of the window.

7

NESSA

Well there's no need to tell Ewan why I think a spell for a love potion will be absolutely useless to me at the moment.

There's only one person I'd be interested in loving, and he's all loved up with a bad-attitude blonde trollop who hates me.

I hate her as well, so we're at least even on that score.

'Tell me more about the witches we're visiting today,' I say, after a bit. The conversation has dried up a little after the love potions comment. Also, I kind of like hearing his voice, and the acoustics in Winnie, who is basically a glorified tin-box, make it sound even richer and darker. He's got a voice like cocoa in a mug on a cold winter's evening. I could snuggle up with that voice, no problem. It's the perfect Halloween voice and it's nearly Halloween and . . .

'Well, you know about Maggie, the witch that never was,' he says, turning away from the window and facing me, interrupting my wicked thoughts about snuggling up to him, 'but you don't know about Kincladie Woods, do you?'

'I don't,' I say.

'There were eight witches strangled, then burned at the stake in 1662, in those woods,' says Ewan, 'and not an Agnes amongst them.' He flips open his notebook and reads out the list of names. 'Issobel McKendley, Elspeth Reid, Jonet Toyes, Jonet Airth, Helen IIson, Margret Crose, Jonet Martin and Jonet Young. You might be interested to know,' he says, turning the page, 'that two Agnes's were tried but not executed, so they must have been innocent. Agnes Ramsay and Agnes Hutsone.'

'Hurrah for the Agnes's,' I say ironically.

'There's also a rumour that some other witches were drowned in the River Earn.'

'That's a wee bit further north, isn't it?'

'It is,' agrees Ewan. 'Runs right into the Tay and then into the North Sea.'

'So the ashes would have travelled a long, long way,' I say. 'It's a bit scary.'

'It's not pleasant.'

'I think my great-great-grandmother was lucky she didn't exist in those days,' I say. 'I've often said she would have been executed as well.'

'I hope you're not studying the darker side of magic, with your book and everything.'

'No,' I say emphatically, 'it's all about Wicca and nature spirits, the sort of thing I'm looking at. Oh — is this the turning here?'

'I believe it is,' says Ewan. And we head towards Dunning and Maggie Wall.

EWAN

We drive through a small, pretty village with stone cottages and whitewashed pubs lining the narrow road. Winnie edges her way expertly through the lanes and out the other side, then we turn left at a crossroads and trundle off towards the monument.

Purple and green mountains seem to herald our way on the left and I can see more of the same in the far distance to the right. We pass a collection of farm buildings and suddenly I can see the monument perched on its cairn of stones with the big cross sitting atop.

There's a narrow grass verge that Nessa swings Winnie onto. Schubert gives a yowl of protest and a soft *flumpf* makes me think he's rolled over in the cat carrier and hit the sides.

''Maggie Wall, burnt here, 1657, as a witch',' reads Nessa. The words are painted white and lie stark against the grey, lichen-covered post. Despite myself, I shiver slightly. I know this monument is probably a folly and all that, but this really did happen to people. I chance a glance over at Nessa and she is staring at the monument, perhaps thinking the same thing as I am.

'All right?' I ask.

'Yes, thanks,' she replies, a little tightly. 'Well, come on, then. Let's go and have a look. Then we might have a cup of tea.'

Of course. I keep forgetting we're in a camper van. A home from home — and fully equipped as one too. And a cup of tea sounds rather nice. Sort of normal and pleasant.

'Good idea.'

Nessa nods and gets out of the van. She hops down to the road and thrusts her hands in her pockets, then stomps up the four steps to the enclosure the monument is in. She walks up to it and stares at it for a moment, then slowly circles the thing looking at the big, square blocks the cairn is made out of. I follow her and wait for her to complete her circuit.

'Someone's been here to put offerings on the stones,' she says. She stands next to me and we both stare at the debris which has been pushed into the crevasses. Candles, flowers, crystals, horrible little Halloween dolls, pumpkins and decapitated-head key-rings fill the holes. I think it looks awful, personally.

'It looks awful, doesn't it?' she says.

'It does,' I agree. 'There's no need for it. It's all rubbish.'

'I think most of it has been put here with good intentions,' muses Nessa. She leans over and plucks a bat with googly eyes and vile rubber wings out of the masonry and looks at it in distaste. 'But crap like this needs to be removed.' She flicks the thing away and it bounces over the fence and into the farmer's field. 'Ritual litter, with the emphasis on 'litter',' she says.

'Not something you would do, then?' I ask her.

'Not here,' she says. 'I tied a ribbon

around a tree in Glastonbury when Winnie and I went there, but that's different. The things here — they're just wrong.'

'Apparently the villagers aren't too fond of it either,' I tell her. 'Geoff says so in his book. They have to tidy it all away, you know.'

'Well I'm sure they get fed up doing that,' she says. 'Come on. We're Maggie's guests and the least we can do is help. I'll go and get a plastic bag from Winnie.'

She turns on her heel and stomps off towards the camper van, her boots making a squelching sound on the soggy, well-trodden grass.

I consider picking the rubber bat up out of the field and then think I had better stop considering it and do it — heaven forbid the farmer sees it there and thinks we've been adding to the ritual litter. So I lean over the fence and reach across for it. As I'm leaning, I can sense Nessa coming up behind me and hear her breathing. I straighten up to speak to her.

Then I see Nessa at the far end of the compound making her way down the steps of the camper van and shaking a plastic bag out, a frown on her face.

God knows who just breathed on me, then, but it scares the hell out of me when I realise it wasn't her.

8

NESSA

'Are you all right?' I ask Ewan. I shake the bag out and it inflates with the wind that's just blown up from the fields and rushed past me. It's like having a Marks and Spencer's branded kite in my hands.

'Fine, thanks,' he says, but he doesn't look fine. He's quite pale and blinking a lot. It's not a good look for a six foot three rugby player.

'Did Maggie come to say hello?' I ask him. I try to make a joke, but it makes him look even more terrified. Then he sort of composes himself and smiles.

'I doubt it,' he says. 'She's a fake, remember?'

'Oh yes,' I say and grin at him. 'Ready to do some ritual cleansing, then?'

'More than ready.'

The first thing to go in the bag is that horrible bat and then we systematically remove everything else as well.

I might have felt guilty but I don't. Like I said, it's all ritual litter and this place doesn't need it. It's beautiful, it's natural and it should be as Nature intended it to be; just stone and earth and sky.

'What are we going to do with it all?' Ewan asks, as we put the final item, a rotting banana skin, into the bag. I look at the bag with some distaste. I haven't thought that far ahead.

'Put it in a waste bin?' I suggest. 'There's bound to be one in the village.'

'Good idea,' says Ewan. He looks down the road we just drove along and I can see him calculating distances.

'I suppose we could walk to the village,' he says. 'We have plenty of time. Unless you need to be back home for anything?'

'I'm in no hurry,' I tell him, and gosh isn't that the truth? Extend the day trip with Ewan or go back home? Tough choice. Besides, if anyone sees us together, they'll think we're a 'couple' as opposed to just a couple of individual people, which is quite nice.

I wish that we could spin our day out just that little bit longer, because if I only have Ewan Grainger for one day, I want to make it last as long as I bloody well can.

So, on that basis: 'I have to consider Schubert,' I tell him. 'We can't leave him in Winnie alone and I forgot to bring his lead. I'm not happy to let him out without it just now. Not until he gets his bearings.' He gives me puzzled, but not unkind, sort of look; but he's bound to have seen me taking Schubert around the streets on it for a little exercise so I don't justify it in any way. 'But an alternative,' I continue, 'is that you could spend a little more time with Maggie here, do some writing and jot down your plot whilst I read my book. Winnie is equipped for light snacks so we'll be fine for a little while. At least a couple of hours. Then,' I say, 'I'd like to see Kincladie Woods before we head home.'

There — that should keep him occupied for some time, shouldn't it?

Ewan processes the information and I see him look back at the monument a little longingly.

'That sounds like it might work,' he says. 'Which book are you going to read whilst I work? And can you bear having that rubbish in Winnie for that length of time?' He nods at the bag which is all lumpy and bumpy and doesn't float like a kite any more.

'My Wicca book. And I'll leave this rubbish outside Winnie,' I tell him. 'I'm not contaminating her by having it inside.' I shake my head emphatically. 'No. I don't like the stuff we collected and I don't want it anywhere near Winnie. Does that make me a crazy person?'

'Definitely not,' he says. I'm pleased to see that worried look he had before has gone now and there is, oh my, a twinkle in those eyes. My legs go a little weak and I have to press my knees together to stop myself from tumbling into a panting heap at his feet. 'It makes you sensible,' he continues, leaning in towards me a little. He lowers his voice and I make a tiny squeak somewhere in my throat as he comes close to me. Then he grins. 'I can smell that banana peel from here.'

EWAN

Okay, so the banana peel thing wasn't the most sensible comment to make under the circumstances, but my god, I can smell it and it's disgusting.

For a moment, when I was getting closer to Nessa and I was right up to her, I definitely felt a little spark between us and she just looked so gorgeous with her green eyes all wide and innocent and not a bit of craziness about her at all.

Then I checked myself, because the

last thing I want to do is force myself upon her when she knows I've got a girlfriend.

I have to say, though, that the idea of Fern as a girlfriend is getting less and less appealing as the day goes on.

Nessa is funny and quirky and innocent and Fern is none of those things. In fact, I'm starting to wonder what I saw in Fern in the first place? Yes, she looked pretty damn good in a gold lamé bikini, and she seemed to be happy for me as my career took off — but apart from that . . .

As if on cue, my mobile phone beeps and I take it out of my pocket. And what do you know: it's Fern.

Hey babes, what you up to? Miss you!

I pull a face and glare at it. I'm conscious of Nessa looking at me and she must have seen my face change.

She says softly, 'Hadn't you better answer her?'

'She knows where I am.'

'Bet she doesn't know I'm here

though,' says Nessa tartly. I dart a quick glance up to her and she looks like an evil imp.

'So what if you are?'

Then my phone goes again.

Just swung by your house to pop those Caribbean brochures through your letterbox. Think that stupid cat is on your roof again. I can hear it.

Without thinking, I text back *It's not Schubert. He's perfectly safe, don't worry.*

I don't mention the brochures. I think she has some idea of enticing me over there for a romantic break or, in Fern World, a 'surprise' engagement or wedding that would only be a surprise to me.

How do you know about the cat? she fires back.

Okay, I'm fed up with this now. I quickly turn the phone to silent mode as this text conversation could get very annoying and the bleeps are simply spoiling the peace of the countryside. Then the screen flashes silently yet angrily as Fern decides to ring instead and I groan.

I press the button to answer and just as I do, Nessa, who now has her back to me, begins to walk away and starts making some comment about how she thinks lying trollops should get what's coming to them and for one horrible moment there is silence on the end of the line and I hope Fern hasn't heard her.

Then Fern's voice comes through, falsely bright and a little strained. 'Where are you? Will you back tonight? Who are you with?'

And then Nessa, who is a little way away by now, bursts into song, belting out that old number about love potion number nine.

'Tra la la,' she bellows tunelessly. Then, in an equally loud voice, she says, 'Agnes was accused of using one you know. I wonder if they work? Maybe Maggie Wall can tell us, or maybe we can ask the ghosts of those witches in Kincladie Woods. Come on,

Ewan, let's find out. Oh bugger, didn't realise you were on the phone.' She looks genuinely shocked to see me there with it against my ear. 'Did they hear my singing? Oh dear!'

'Yes I should be back tonight,' I say into the phone, still looking at Nessa who has gone white and mouths 'Fern?'

Fern in her turn gabbles something incoherent about me not telling her anything and using her and everything else and blah blah blah.

'Just stop it,' I say. 'Nessa gave me a lift, my car broke down. What's the problem?'

'She's the problem!' squawks Fern. Then she hangs up on me.

'Whoopsie,' says Nessa. She shifts that disgusting bag from one hand to the other and looks at me. 'Do you want to head back, then?'

It might be my imagination, but she sounds a little sad.

'Of course not. Fern is overreacting. I don't know what her problem is.'

'Why should there be a problem?' Nessa asks. 'I'm not half as pretty as her. She has no need to worry.'

'Don't put yourself down!' I snap. Then I have to clamp my lips shut before I say something that will change the dynamics of the day and send Nessa hurtling back into the driving seat of Winnie, where she will roar off into the distance and leave me stranded with Maggie Wall.

I have to stop myself from saying that I, personally, find Nessa far more attractive than Fern. Which is wholly inappropriate.

Nessa would never be interested in me. And I have a girlfriend anyway.

That last phrase actually depresses me.

9

NESSA

I didn't know Fern was on the phone, honest I didn't. But Ewan is right. Why should it be a problem that I'm here? We're here as friends, as companions. I gave him a lift. End of.

And you know what? He deserves so much better than someone like her anyway. From what I understand, she's needy, she's high maintenance and she lies to the press about innocent people.

She's not a nice person.

And I don't think she's an animal lover, either. Schubert is an excellent judge of character and he likes Ewan but he can't stand Fern. I can see it in his eyes and the way that his fur bristles up when she's nearby.

Which reminds me — he's surely ready to get out of his basket now and have a sniff around. He doesn't really need his lead around here, does he? Anyway, there are bound to be field mice or shrews or the like in those farmer's fields that he'll enjoy running after.

I head back to Winnie and leave the grotty bag on the grass outside the door. I climb up into the van and pick up Schubert's carrier. I take him outside and set the carrier down by the edge of the field.

I open the flap and direct him to the fields. 'Go on, Schubert. Off you go. Ten minutes run around and then come back, okay?'

He's normally pretty good and does what he's told, but today he just looks at me and goes 'Mow wow,' which is Schubert for 'No thanks.' I tilt the basket and shake it a bit and he slides forward, but I can see him digging his claws in to the blanket in the hope it will pin him in place.

'Mow *wow!*' he says again, which is Schubert for 'leave me the hell alone or

I shall scratch your eyes out.'

'Okay,' I say tetchily. 'I'll just leave you here, then. You can pop out if you want. We'll be here for a bit longer.' I throw a glance at Ewan. 'Won't we?' I ask.

'Yes we will,' he says, and he smiles at me. 'Will he be okay there if we go inside? Or do you want us to sit outside?'

I want us to go inside, lock the doors, pull the chintz curtains too and roll around naked on the twin bunk that converts to a double.

'He'll be fine. We can sit out or in, your choice,' I say, carefully.

Ewan looks up at the sky. There are a few clouds building up over the mountains, but they seem to be hanging there and not doing too much else. There's a bit of a breeze blowing up and it might get chilly though.

'Outside for a bit,' says Ewan. 'This scenery is too good to miss. Plenty of time to sit inside if that storm heads over. Agreed?'

'Agreed,' I say. I have a couple of folding chairs and a folding table for just such an occasion, so we pull them outside and set them up on the verge overlooking Maggie Wall and the distant mountains.

'I hope nobody else wants to visit the monument today,' I say. 'We've sort of taken over the grass.'

'It'll be fine,' says Ewan. 'Now, will you show me how to boil a kettle in this thing and I'll treat you to a cuppa. It's the least I can do to thank you for bringing me here.'

'My pleasure.' I can feel myself blushing and going girly and just restrain myself from giggling like Scarlett O'Hara at Rhett Butler. 'This way.'

I show him where everything is and it feels kind of domestic and nice and I like it.

I really don't want to have to head home this evening. I've enjoyed spending time with Ewan.

And he's not bad on the eyes either, which is a bonus.

EWAN

I get a shedload of work done, sitting on that grassy roadside with the occasional car going past. The storm has held off and it's turned out to be one of those lovely, crisp autumn days that fill your lungs with the fresh air and make you feel glad to be alive.

Nessa is sitting in the other chair reading her Wicca book. She has her feet up on the table, crossed at the ankles, and every so often she twists one of her curls into a tight little sausage then lets it spring back into shape before she turns the page.

'May I borrow a pen and some paper?' she asks at one point.

'No,' I say, and laugh when she snaps her head up like an angry meercat. 'You can't borrow the paper,' I clarify. 'You'll have to keep that, because it's no good to me once you've written on it. But yes, you can borrow a pen. I always travel well-equipped.'

'Oh!' she says, then sticks her tongue

out at me. 'Never tangle with an author.' She drawls it out so it sounds like 'awwww-thuuuurrrrr'. She reaches over, takes the pen and paper and for the briefest moment our fingertips connect. I don't know if she feels the little fizz of electricity that shoots up my arm, or whether it's just me — but there is the tiniest pause. Then: 'Thank you, Ewan,' she says and ducks her head down to jot something on to the paper.

The *zing* throws me off balance a little. I stare at my notebook and the pages I've filled in the last couple of hours. The story is heading in a great direction, but I seriously don't know what's going to happen in it myself.

A bit like life, I suppose.

'Nessa,' I say, curiously.

'Hmmm?' she replies, her attention still on her Wicca book.

'Are you a planner or a winger?'

'What?' She looks at me and pulls a face. 'A winger? What does that mean?'

'Do you just wing it in life or do you

plan things out?' It sounds a bit daft, saying it aloud, but Nessa doesn't seem to take it that way.

She tilts her chin up and seems to be thinking. 'I wing it,' she says eventually. 'Yes. Yes, I do. I didn't even plan where I wanted to work — there was an advert in the window of the building when I went past it. And it was a nice-looking building so I went in and applied for the job on the spot.'

'But didn't you need a CV or something?' I ask, slightly confused.

'I think I was meant to have one but I didn't have one with me but Mr Hogarth said he liked me turning up just on spec, he thought I had a good spunky attitude — '

'*Spunky?*' I almost choke on the word. What sort of word is *that* to use nowadays?

'Spunky,' clarifies Nessa, without missing a beat, 'so I got the job. And even though I knew I wanted to move out from my parents' house, I had no idea where I was going to live. Then Mr

Hogarth said he knew of somewhere that sounded perfect; and in fact he *knew* it was perfect because he owned it and his godson was very happy there, and the lower apartment just happened to be vacant. I looked at it on the internet, and by tea time I had the place.'

'You hadn't even viewed it?' I ask. 'He didn't need to see references or anything?'

'Nope. Mr Hogarth was happy to proceed, and I don't think I've let him down as a tenant. And nope, I didn't view it. I just liked the look of it.' She waves her hand around vaguely. 'I sort of knew where it was, so I knew it was a nice area. That's all, really.'

'But your flat has a weird staircase in it,' I say, stupidly. 'It takes up a great deal of space in your lounge.'

'Yes. But it leads into your flat, and I like you, so that's fine.' She puts her head back down and turns a page. Then she pops her head back up. 'And I didn't plan to get Schubert. We just found each other. Sometimes, the nicest things are the things you don't plan for.'

'Is that why you got Winnie?' I ask her. 'So you could do a few things without planning ahead?'

'Yes. But again, I didn't plan to buy her. My brother Hugo saw her for sale at the side of the road by the coast and he mentioned it in a text. So I told him to go and get her for me. I paid him back for her, of course and then I went with him to bring her home.' She frowns. 'We only had one breakdown on the way back up, but Hugo's very good with engines so we were fine.

'Anyway, that summer, when I decided to go up and down Britain, I knew where I was going to end up at each end, but I didn't know my journey. That was part of the fun of it.' Then she looks at me straight in the eyes and I wonder if there's a hidden meaning when she says, 'You should try enjoying the journey, you know. There's no need to be railroaded into stuff. Try being a free spirit, Ewan. You might like it.'

Unbidden, an image of Fern pops into my head; Fern with her Caribbean brochures and her control freak ways and her determination to live my life for me.

'You're a free spirit, aren't you?' I ask Nessa.

'Oh well, now, I think I am,' she says. Then suddenly she grins at me. 'I am so free that, on impulse, I need to tell you that it's cup of tea time again. You're nearest the kettle. There's some Hobnobs in the biscuit barrel as well. Chocolate ones.'

'I've never had the chocolate ones.'

'Then you should try them. Live a little,' says Nessa and turns back to her book.

10

NESSA

It's been a very pleasurable few hours, sitting on the roadside with Ewan. I wonder if one day we might be the sort of old couple that unpack a picnic in a parking place by a mountain of road salt, then I realise that we aren't actually a couple and I feel a little sad.

But never mind, we have today at least. Which reminds me that we probably need to make a move if we want to see Kincladie Woods before dark.

As if on cue, there is an almighty rumble from the distant mountains and we both look up. The clouds start to roll towards us and I can see that weird curtain effect coming over the field, which means torrential rain is on the way and it won't be long before we're in the middle of it.

Ewan swears and we jump up and shove everything back into the back of Winnie. I make a dash to rescue Schubert and Ewan takes hold of that awful bag full of ritual litter.

'What do I do with this?' he asks, pulling a face.

'Can you tie it onto the wing mirror?' I ask, placing Schubert and his carrier snugly in the space underneath the bench seats. 'Then it's not being left here and we can find a bin, but it's not going inside Winnie.' I shake my head

'I can't tie it on,' says Ewan, struggling with it a bit. Then I see him looking towards the village. 'Nessa, I'll run to the village with it. It won't take me long. You can pick me up there, okay?'

'Run to the village?' I repeat, 'But it's ages away. How can you run all that way?'

'I'm still pretty fit,' says Ewan with

the ghost of a smile on his lips. 'Although you may not think so.'

Well actually, I *do* think he's pretty fit, although I suspect his and my definitions of 'fit' are probably different but I won't split hairs.

'Ewan!' I say, with some vague hope of trying to stop him. The rain has started now, big fat drops that are splashing onto the road and obscuring my view from the windows. I look around the interior of Winnie but there is absolutely nowhere I want that bag. 'Ewan . . . ' I say again, rather pathetically.

'Race you!' he says and he's off.

Oh my. He *is* fit.

I hurry into the driver's seat and start Winnie up. She chokes once or twice then gets herself sorted. And before I know it, we are off in some crazy race and Ewan is actually winning for the first part of it.

I can barely concentrate on my driving for watching him. He's just streaking along the road and he doesn't seem to care that he's getting soaking wet. His hair is plastered to his head, but it's so short anyway that it doesn't look silly. His white shirt is clinging to his body *á la* Mr Darcy as well and oh my, that's not a bad sight either because I can see each and every muscle defined as he pumps his arms and runs. And I can see that sneaky little tattoo through the damp material. Oh *my*.

'Meooow!' comes an agitated noise from the back.

'Sorry, Schubert!' I shout. 'Didn't mean to swerve like that.' And I didn't — I just wanted to get a bit closer to Ewan.

Oh dear. I've overtaken him now. I look out of my wing mirror and see him pounding along. He looks up and gives me a grin and a little wave.

I should ask him to take my rubbish away more often.

I wonder if he would run down our staircase and look like that?

Hmmm. It's a thought.

EWAN

Nessa is already out of the van and waiting for me when I arrive at the village. She's soaking well as well, due to the fact that she's been standing on the roadside, in the rain, for the last few minutes waving at me. As I approach, she leans into Winnie and pops out again, hiding something behind her back.

'Next time,' I tell her, drawing to a halt in front of her, 'you can do the running. I did it to save you getting wet and it clearly hasn't worked.' I can't help smiling at her though. She looks so sweet and vulnerable with her hair all plastered to her face like that and her scarf plopping great globs of water onto the tarmac.

Nessa laughs and her arms appear from behind her. She drops something over my head — I realise that it's one of those Hawaiian garlands. I don't know what else she has in the bowels of Winnie.

'Have the winner's LuaLua,' she says triumphantly. 'You've just achieved a gold medal in the Dunning Maggie-athlon.'

'I think you mean winner's lei,' I tell her, smiling. 'LuaLua is a footballer.'

'Oh,' she says and blinks. 'Fancy you knowing that. Now I know why I got a funny look in the shop when I asked to buy a LuaLua. Why didn't Scott tell me?'

'Scott?'

'My brother,' she says. 'You know. The one who did my decorating? The interior designer? I asked his advice on decorating Winnie. He was with me on LuaLua day.'

'Ah,' I say, stupidly. Nessa has a butterfly mind and I'm clearly not as random in my thoughts as she is. 'Why *didn't* he tell you, I wonder?'

She shrugs. 'Probably because he's my brother. But I don't want to talk about Scott. I want to talk about you. You're very fit.' Then I almost swear that she blushes and, as if she wants to hide it, she makes a big deal about looking around and her gaze finally settles on a large public bin a few metres away.

She points to it. 'Bin,' she says. 'We can dump the litter. Then what?' She turns back to face me and blinks. 'Kincladie? Or can't you handle a haunted wood?'

'I can handle a haunted wood, all right,' I say. 'But it's still raining.'

'Hmm. So it is.'

'It might not be very nice walking in the woods in the rain.'

'It might not be,' she concedes.

I am conscious of her looking me up and down and I think I must look like something Schubert dragged in.

'You look like something Schubert dragged in,' she says. 'You can dry off in Winnie or we can go to the pub for something to eat. My treat. Or we can quickly see the woods then head home. It's only water after all and we're both relatively damp. Fern might be wanting you for something anyway. Maybe she needs you to pour bleach on her follicles.'

Her tone is acerbic and I shouldn't but I feel a smile twitching at the corner of my mouth. And then I see that there's a pub just along the road and it looks like one of those nice country ones where the log fire will be roaring.

I give the matter some thought for all of a millisecond and quash a vision of Fern and her waspish mouth pursed into something resembling Schubert's bum. It overlays with a vision of me and Nessa, who incidentally has a perfectly lovely soft and kissable mouth, lounging in a country pub together in the chilly October dusk. It's a dangerous decision and there can be only one answer.

'Pub,' I say. 'We might dry off by the fire. Then we can visit the woods when it's darker. Really soak up the atmosphere.'

'As opposed to being literally soaked out here?' says Nessa. 'Good idea. But dump that litter first, please.'

She smiles at me, pushes a lock of

wet hair out of her face and turns away, walking up the little street towards the pub. Winnie looks incongruous, parked in such a little old-fashioned village. But none of us, including Winnie, seem to care.

'But what about Schubert?' I shout after her.

'He doesn't like pubs,' she shouts back over her shoulder. 'He said he didn't want to come. And anyway, Catnip is underage. Schubert's got his food, he's got his milk and he's wandering around in Winnie and he'll be fine. He won't escape.'

And it's only as we walk into the pub, that I realise I'm still wearing the Hawaiian garland.

NESSA

Ewan draws a couple of odd looks from the clientele, but it doesn't bother me. Neither, it seems, does it bother the barman who is quite taken by the lei and asks Ewan all about it.

'Did you two just come back from Hawaii then?' he asks. 'Looks like the weather wasn't that kind to you.' Then he laughs like it's the funniest thing in the world.

'No, we didn't come from Hawaii,' I tell him. 'We came from Edinburgh but we visited Maggie Wall and Ewan got wet as he was trying to dispose of the litter from the monument. We spent ages tidying it up.'

'You got rid of all that stuff?' asked the barman. 'Don't tell me, your boyfriend found the lei in amongst it.' He shakes his head sadly. 'The rubbish they leave. They just don't think.'

'Oh no, the lei is from my camper van,' I tell him. 'They didn't put it on the monument, don't worry about that.'

The barman perks up. 'In that case, drinks are on the house. What do you two fancy, then?'

I am desperate to say that I fancy Ewan. I settle on lemonade.

I don't bother to correct the barman

103

about Ewan not being my boyfriend either.

I wonder if Ewan noticed?

EWAN

I think I could easily fancy Nessa. But there's no way I'd say anything.

So I smile and order a coke and don't correct the barman about the girlfriend comment.

I wonder if she noticed?

Anyway, we're warm and dry now at least; and we'll soon be contentedly stuffed full of food as well, because we've ordered dinner.

It's so relaxing being with Nessa like this. We've never been anywhere together, despite the fact we've lived beside each other for three years and spoken almost every day. I think I would miss her if she wasn't there anymore. I can't imagine living anywhere without Nessa and not having Schubert around.

That's pretty weird, isn't it? Surely it should be Fern I'm thinking about like that? But it's not. It's Nessa.

I cast a glance over in her direction and she's looking around the place with interest.

Then she says: 'Oh no. Wrong pub.'

'Why is this the wrong pub?' I ask. 'It's a very nice pub.'

'Oh yes it is,' replies Nessa, 'but it's not where Maggie's skull is.'

Then my neurons fire; they must have dried out a bit to make that happen. 'Ah! Yes, I remember that from the book,' I say. 'Where was it now? Let me check.' I pull out my phone as I have Maggie's e-book downloaded onto that as well. 'The Saracen's Head in Glasgow,' I say a few moments later.

'That's the one,' says Nessa. 'I saw it in the book yesterday. It's quite a long way from here, though, isn't it? If it *is* her skull.'

'Again,' I say, shrugging, 'who knows if it's her or not. It's a nice legend though.'

'And if the pub is called The Saracen's Head, who's to say it's not simply a Saracen? Maybe Maggie was a Saracen? It's confusing. But Ewan, don't let them put my skull on display, will you?' she says. 'Because when I die, that paparazzi guy will no doubt break into my coffin and display it on a spike. Fern will probably tip him off when I go and tell him where to find me. Maybe I should be cremated instead. Rather than being burnt at the stake. That would, work, wouldn't it?'

I think she's probably only half joking. 'Well whatever happens, they can't find us today,' I say. 'They don't know we're here.'

'Thank goodness for that!' Nessa says and grins. She leans forward and I can see a spark of excitement in her eyes. 'I'm looking forward to seeing these woods. Should be *very* atmospheric. It is almost Halloween after all.'

'You're sure you're not going to be scared?'

'Me?' she replies and opens her eyes

wide. 'Why should I be scared? Agnes will look after me and fend the evil spirits off. And if she doesn't, I'll do it myself. Why, I'm half way through my book so I'm practically qualified. Ewan, do you think I could be a necromancer?'

I almost choke on my coke, and for the first time I'm a little unnerved by Nessa and her witchcraft. I think it has something to do with the fact her hair has dried all wild and curly, and the firelight is highlighting part of her face and leaving other bits in the dark, and the flames are flickering in her eyes and she's looking straight at me and I can't look away . . .

And my God, she's gorgeous.

Is this how people get seduced by witches — they genuinely get bewitched?

Bloody hell.

'Ewan?' she says and I realise I've drifted off into some fantasy world where Nessa is dressed in a tight, corseted black dress with a split right up to the thigh revealing long, black boots, and she's sitting provocatively on a broomstick and Schubert is a true witch's familiar — a sleek, purring genius of the feline variety . . .

'Ewan!' she says again, more sharply. I blink and suddenly she's just Nessa again. And a confused-looking waiter is hovering by the table.

'Hunter's chicken?' he says. 'And cod and chips?'

'Me!' we both say, raising our hands at the same time. Then we look at each other and we laugh and the waiter laughs with us and then he puts the food down and it's all normal again.

But I'm still thinking about Nessa's legs and that black dress . . .

11

NESSA

Well my hunter's chicken was divine. I think Ewan enjoyed his fish and chips as well, and I must say we were both very, very quiet when we were eating. And our food didn't last long and that's always an indication of good food.

He did take the LuaLua off before he ate, which I thought was quite well-mannered. Then he put it on again afterwards, which shows he has an excellent sense of humour.

Like I told him, it's my treat, so I'm currently at the bar paying and wondering exactly how much longer I can stretch our trip out for. I know we're off to Kincladie Woods now but somehow it's not enough for me.

Does that make me a bad person?

But there's not much else to do, once we've done the woods.

If only . . .

I wish . . .

'All right?' Ewan's voice is just next to my ear. I jump slightly and turn to see him bending down to murmur the question to me. For a moment I just stare at him, at his mouth and his eyes and I just enjoy being so close to him.

'I don't — ' I start, then I clamp my lips together. I want to say that I don't want to go home, or I don't want him to go back to Fern or I don't want to just leave this magical day behind and have us still just 'friends' at the end of it. But obviously I can't say any of that. So I change it.

'I don't want Schubert to feel left out.' I say. So I add a packet of prawn cocktail crisps to the bill, and tell Ewan that they're Schubert's favourite. Which is not a lie. It's just not what I wanted to tell Ewan.

'I'd have put him down as more of a

cheese and onion guy, myself,' says Ewan, looking at the crisps.

'No, they make his breath smell,' I tell Ewan, 'so he's not allowed them.'

I pick up the crisps and put my purse away and head towards the door. Ewan slips in front of me and opens it like a gentleman and then we both stop and stare.

It's almost pitch black outside and those clouds we saw over the mountains have reached the village to make a thick fog which blankets everything.

I hadn't realised we'd spent so much time in the pub.

'Well now, Kincladie Woods are going to be fun in this!' I say.

'Yep,' agrees Ewan. His voice sounds oddly muffled in the fog. 'Come on — race you to Winnie.' He sprints off and I falter a little, then sprint after him, shouting at him in the hope of putting him off. His laugh disappears into the fog and I run faster.

I hate running, I really do.

But it's the principle of the thing.

And I have the keys. So ha ha, Ewan Grainger — even if you get there first, it isn't going to help you!

EWAN

Nessa is not very good at running. She pitches up gasping and choking a few minutes after me and bends double next to Winnie.

'You. Win,' she coughs out. After a few minutes, she stands up. I realise that I've been rubbing her back as she recovers herself. It seems like the most natural thing in the world, but I take my hand away as soon as I realise that I'm doing it.

'All right?' I ask again and she nods.

'I have the keys anyway,' she says and produces them. They dangle from the end of her finger and then she flips them into her palm and unlocks the door.

A black ball of fur leaps out and jumps right into Nessa's arms, closely followed by a purr that sounds like a chainsaw.

'I know, I missed you too,' she says and puts the cat down. We both climb into Winnie and it's surprisingly warm and cosy in here, especially when Nessa clicks on the light. Not only do the normal lights come on, but so does a net of tiny stars which criss-cross the ceiling. The colours of the patchwork blankets she has over the seats, the strangely patterned hairy wool crocheted footstool cover and the contrasting cushions scattered around make the place look really welcoming and she's also got a strange, mismatched collection of bright china in the lime-green wall cupboards. It looks a bit like a Jasper Conran/Habitat advert from the eighties. But it's nice. I like it. I add the lei to the décor by hanging it on the corner of what I assume is a wardrobe — and I must admit that it does look good.

Nessa straightens up, having opened the crisps and scattered them on a blue and white willow pattern saucer, and smiles at me.

'Winnie comes alive at night, doesn't she?' she asks, as if she knows what I've just been thinking. 'The colours always look so much brighter, somehow. I don't know if it's the lightbulbs.' She squints up at one and frowns. Then she shrugs her shoulders. 'It might be. I always wanted a gypsy caravan you know. But I tried one once and me and the horse didn't get on. I told Billy — '

' — your brother?'

' — my brother, that it wasn't for me, so he took it back to the seller for me and made an excuse. I didn't know you knew Billy. He's a car salesman, but he always seems to know where to get good bargains in the transport world.'

It hardly seems worth suggesting she could have tried a different horse.

'So I might just get a gypsy caravan and put it in the garden if I ever get a garden big enough. I'll have to see,' Nessa continues. 'Oh, good *boy*, Schubert. You've eaten them all up.

Okay — I think we're ready to see Kincladie Woods now. *Whoooooo*!' she makes fluttery motions with her hands as if to indicate a ghost. 'Let's see if we can scare Ewan.' Then she winks at me and climbs into the driver's seat.

'Impossible,' I tell her, climbing through to the front after her. 'Oh — what about the lights?' I half-turn to go back and switch them off, but she shakes her head. 'No, it's fine. Leave them on. If Schubert wants them off, he'll do it. You see the kitchen unit?'

'Yes?' I say faintly.

'He can climb on there and reach the switch with his paw. He's done it before.'

We are about half a mile down the road, almost at the woods, when the lights in the back of Winnie go off. We are plunged into darkness and there is a soft sound and a 'Mow wow,' as if a substantially sized cat has landed on a hairy wool crocheted covered footstool.

Then there is the contented sigh as said cat snuggles into a mouse-shaped toy and then a quiet dragging as he pulls it closer to him.

NESSA

I don't think Ewan realised Schubert could switch the light out. It's one of the many things Schubert can do. He's pretty clever for a cat, I must admit. I've never trained him as such, he just does things and works it all out for himself.

I just wish he wasn't so opinionated at times.

Anyway, we're just about approaching Kincladie Woods now, and it is very, very atmospheric.

'Wow', I say, as I pull Winnie up to yet another grass verge, just before we reach the wood properly. It seems to be a thick, dense grouping of awfully big trees. Kincladie Woods doesn't look massively scary at this point, but when I checked the map earlier, I saw that it's quite a substantial area so who knows what it's like further in?

There's a car tucked into the only space that's really decent enough to fit a vehicle, just along the road by the woods. Then I see a little road leading to the left and it seems to run alongside the edge of Kincladie, so I turn Winnie up there instead. It's that or the other verge and because it is so dark now, who's to say there isn't a ditch? Winnie can do many things, but clambering out of ditches is not one of them.

This is how I justify our trespassing to Ewan as he starts to protest, anyway.

'There might be a ditch on the other side,' I tell him, 'so we'll park along here.'

'But it's dark and this might be private land.'

'And maybe it's not private land,' I tell him. I feel a little triumphant.

'It's much darker around here, don't you think?' Ewan asks me as I stop Winnie and kill the engine. Suddenly, we're simply surrounded by silence and velvety blackness. The fog that was coming in before is hanging around here like an unwelcome relation at Christmas, and despite my bravado, I shiver, just a little.

I'm quite glad Ewan is with me, to be honest. There's something strange here that I just can't quite put my finger on. As if he agrees, Schubert creeps forward and paws my lap.

I lift him up and cuddle him. 'So do you still fancy looking around the woods?' I ask Ewan.

'Yes,' he says, 'I definitely do. I think this will be a great setting for part of my book'.

I cast a sidelong glance at him under cover of snuggling into Schubert's fur. 'Yes,' I reply, and my voice has an oddly hollow sound to it, loud in the complete stillness of the world outside. 'I'm still not scared, you know,' I say. And do you know what, it's true; having thought about it, I'm not scared.

I'm just very, very interested to see what secrets this place feels fit to share with us tonight.

12

EWAN

Nessa has chosen the perfect place to park Winnie up. There is no way anyone can find us here unless they are looking for us and let's face it, that's highly unlikely. Who would even expect two reprobates like Nessa and I to be poking around at the site of a seventeenth-century mass execution?

Because basically, that's what it is.

'Those ladies were probably innocent,' Nessa says, her voice soft in the warm, dry confines of Winnie. 'It's very sad.'

'Very true,' I say. 'Well. Shall we go and explore?'

'Yes, let's.' She attempts to put Schubert down on the ground, but encounters some issues as he's hooked his claws into her sweater. She eventually disentangles the beast and he glares at her and gives one of those 'Mow wow' comments that she swears is his way of communicating.

'Now don't be silly, Schubert,' she says. 'It's perfectly safe.'

Schubert remains unimpressed and stalks to the back of Winnie with his tail in the air. Then he suddenly pauses and tilts his head to the side as if he's listening to something. Then he stalks back to the door and just stands there, looking at it.

'Schubert, out of the way.'

'Mow wow,' says Schubert.

'Well, all right,' says Nessa. 'You can have ten minutes out there to stretch your legs as well. You haven't had a lot of fresh air today, have you?' She points her finger at him and wags it. 'But you had your chance earlier, so you can't complain, all right?'

'Mow wow,' says Schubert and again I look at him in confusion.

Nessa opens the door and the cat

disappears into the night.

'Our turn now,' says Nessa. She steps out of the camper van without, it seems, a second thought, and I pull on my hooded jacket and follow her.

Kincladie Woods are the oddest place. I have been to many strange locations in my time, but this spot, on a foggy night near Halloween is indescribable — and a lack of coherent words is never good for an author.

Nessa and I walk towards a gap in the trees where the forest seems to swallow itself up in swampy, dark green gulps and we push through some shrubs. I want to reach out and take her hand to guide her through the place, but I shove my hands in my pockets instead. Her breath comes in sweet little puffs as she scrambles over some fallen logs and although I can't see her too clearly, there is a reassuring warmth about the fact that soon she is walking along next to me again.

'Did you bring a torch?' she asks. 'I don't think the moon is going to get through this canopy very well, especially with the fog.'

'I've got one on my phone,' I tell her.

'I've got one like that too,' she says. 'Do you think we should switch them on?'

'Yes — but one at a time,' I say. 'They'll drain the batteries and we can't afford to lose all the light at once.'

'There's a torch in the van.' Her voice is muted and I think that's the combined effect of the fog and the trees. 'I can go back and get it, if you like?'

'I think we're fine for the moment.'

'Okay,' she says easily, and I can sense her shrugging her shoulders, rather than *seeing* her shrug them, 'just let me know if you want me to. I can easily go back. It's no bother. I can — '

Then there's a God almighty yowl from somewhere way in front of us and a strangled 'Mow wooooowwwwwww!'

'*Schubert!*' Nessa screams, and then she sprints way ahead of me, disappearing into the forest with a terrible crashing and snapping of twigs and branches.

'Nessa!' I yell — but it's too late. She's gone and all I can see is the blackness of the forest and all I can hear is the sighing of the wind around me.

It's like she's never been here.

13

NESSA

If Schubert hasn't killed himself, I will probably do it for him if that shout didn't mean anything more than an owl flew too close to him. But I just can't take the chance.

I don't even know where I'm going through these woods. I'm just following what I hope is a path and luckily I've not fallen over and broken my ankle yet; which is usually what happens in horror movies when people are running through haunted forests near Halloween.

I don't really have time to contemplate that too much. I don't even think I have time to do anything more than just run and hope for the best.

'Mow wow.'

I hear Schubert again, but there is

altogether a different tone to his voice.

'Mow *wow*,' I hear. And then — good grief — is he bloody well *purring?*

I stop and take stock of where I am. I'm in the heart of the forest all right. I wrap my arms around myself and peer around me, quite blindly, because the darkness is so impenetrable here.

'Mow wow.' And it's that complacent sounding noise he makes now, which means that wherever he is and whatever he's doing, he's happy about it.

'Schubert?' I say. I'm not speaking that loudly, but there is a weird echo to my voice, quite unlike there was anywhere else in this wood.

Then there is the snap of a twig just behind me and a cold draught whips around my ankles.

I whirl around and there's an ominous droning coming from beyond the tree line: '*Sin. Dex. Sin. Dex. Sin. Dex.*' The strange words are accompanied by a marching sound — the sound of a group of men heading purposefully my way.

But I can't see anybody.

'*Sin. Dex. Sin Dex. Sin Dex.*'

The sound is getting nearer and my heart begins to pound. I feel dizzy and sick. I feel as if someone has punched me in the stomach with an icy cold fist and I catch my breath on a scream.

'Och, don't you worry about those people,' a cheerful voice says just behind me. 'There was a Roman marching camp right here in the woods. I think it was something to do with Agricola in 83AD. Way before Hadrian and his wall.' There is a heartfelt sigh. 'Wasn't the wall built to keep the Sassenachs out of Scotland? Or was it to keep the Picts out of England? Ah well. History is not my strong point. But yes, just ignore the boys. They'll pass by in a wee moment. I think *you* are more interested in the witches, sweetheart. Am I right?'

I spin around again and see a woman standing there. And the oddest thing is that Schubert is in her arms purring like a machine and looking up at her adoringly. He has his paws around her neck and yes, he is actually wagging his tail, just like a dog. The woman is small and slim, yet delightfully curvy where she *should* be curvy and she has cherry-wood coloured hair and the reason I know all this is because, despite the darkness, she is surrounded by a weird, milky-coloured glow which makes her look as if she's been washed by moonlight and polished in starlight.

I wonder briefly if I should be an author too, the same as Ewan, because I think that is rather a nice description of her.

'Are you the woman from the coffee shop?' I blurt out. It's not the most inspired thing to say to a random stranger in a darkened wood.

Maybe I shouldn't be an author after all.

'You got the book then?' she replies and grins at me. 'Good, I *am* glad.'

Then I have one of those daft lightbulb moments.

'You're not ... Maggie Wall? Are you?'

The woman laughs and she has what I can only describe as an utterly filthy laugh.

'Maggie Wall? Good Lord. No, of course I'm not. She's a total fake, that lassie. No. It's all made up. Fancy that, Schubert. She thought I was Maggie Wall!' Schubert utters an equally filthy type of cat-laugh and looks at me as if I am stupid. 'He's such a lovely cat, isn't he?' says the woman, gazing adoringly at Schubert. 'Still as opinionated as ever, though, aren't you my sweet?'

'Mow wow,' says Schubert, comfortably.

I am slightly dumbfounded at this.

'Why don't you take a good look at me?' says the woman. 'Go on. A very good look. What do you see?' She steps forward and smiles at me encouragingly.

I blink and look at her. I don't even need to squint my eyes because she's still glowing.

Now my heart rate has calmed down a little and I can concentrate better, I take in the dark, curly hair and the mischievous eyes and the total devotion to Schubert. The nose is ever-so-slightly different and her mouth is a little thinner than mine, but there's no mistaking her, now I've seen her properly.

'Agnes?' I whisper.

'The very same,' she says. 'Nice to meet you properly at last.' She holds her hand out to me quite formally, even impeded as she is by Schubert, and I reach out without thinking and take it. It's a rather cold hand, and really quite substantial for what I assume is a ghost-hand, but she has a firm handshake, which is always good.

'Now, I don't have very long as I have to be somewhere.' She blushes an icy pink, the colour of a crystallised rose petal, and lowers her eyelashes. 'A rendezvous that I cannot rearrange, if you understand. I don't want him to go off the boil, so to speak.'

I know I am gawping at her. Good Lord, death has not changed this woman at all, has it?

'But you need to know a couple of things,' she continues serenely, raising her eyes to mine. She's a bit shorter than me too. 'Firstly, the witches they condemned to die here? Don't worry about them — '

'I don't want to see them!' I burst out. I do not, I absolutely do *not* want to see those women swinging from the trees or witness some ghostly effigy of their funeral pyres. Hearing those soldiers and chatting to Aggie is more than enough for one night, thank you very much.

'Oh, you will not see them!' says Aggie. 'They're long gone. They've gone to a better place, as they say. I mean — would *you* want to come back to this place after what they did to them?' A frown crosses her beautifully smooth face. 'Because I'm damn sure I wouldn't.'

'I bet they weren't even witches, were they?' I ask.

'Not in the sense of the Dark Arts, they weren't,' says Aggie. She shrugs — no mean feat with Schubert clinging onto her — and shakes her head sadly. 'They were like you and me. A little bit different, a little bit individual. They had a deeper understanding of certain things. And of course,' that wicked grin again, 'they were exceptionally beautiful. Well. Most of them were exceptionally beautiful; some were ugly old hags, but it is too impolite to name names.'

'Aggie!' I say, quite shocked.

'Now don't pretend you weren't wondering the same thing,' she says.

I can't actually pretend I wasn't, because I was.

'So that's the first bit out of the way,' continues Aggie, 'and now I can move onto the more exciting things.' She beckons me closer, again impeded slightly by Schubert, and as if I'm in a dream I take a couple of steps towards her. There's an awfully cold chill around her, but otherwise she looks rather good for someone who's been dead and buried for the best part of a century.

'I saw your young man earlier,' she says, 'when he was poking around the farmer's field and you were in that contraption with the bed in. Have you put him through his paces yet? You know? With the bed?' She winks at me and there's that filthy laugh again.

'Aggie!'

'Hmmm. I did wonder.' She tilts her head and looks at me critically, leaning her cheek on Schubert's head. He lets out an enormous purr. 'Well, let's not worry about that right now, it'll come. And he's got a very nice rear end, I noticed. I'll talk to you about that too. First of all, though, let's think about the matter in hand. That car by the side of the woods.'

'The car? What about it? And what do you mean by 'it will come' and by talking about Ewan's rear end? You awful, awful great-great-granny! It's just *wrong* to hear an old person talk like that!' I squeak, suddenly coming over all prim and proper.

Aggie mutters something that should never really be said by someone of her standing and great antiquity, then she trundles on. 'I might have been old when I died,' she says, 'but inside I was always like this. That is the fabulous thing about being dead. I can go anywhere, do anything and still look gorgeous. I *do* like the fashions nowadays though, I *must* say.' She grins at me over the top of my cat and shakes her glorious cherry-wood mane out. The moonlight catches it and it shimmers like dark molten lava.

'You have fabulous hair,' I tell her. 'But we all thought it was black, like mine.'

'Sweetie, have you never heard of henna? Wonderful stuff. You should try it. Anyway — the car. This is what we need to do, all right?'

And she takes a step closer to me and

whispers in my ear. 'It's all fine, you know. It's all been planned out — up there — ' she points skywards ' — but we can't do everything for you. A lot of it is to do with positive thinking. But the results will be worth it and he'll really *really* like it. I promise.' She giggles in a lewd fashion.

'Positive thinking?'

'Positive thinking. And a wee bit of magic. Look. Sit here, and I'll go through a few things with you.'

'I do appreciate your time,' I say stiffly, one eye on Schubert who is looking smug, 'but Ewan will be waiting for me and I don't know if it's quite right that he should come across us discussing magic when he thinks I'm saving Schubert's life.'

'My dear girl, I can make time stand still. I can make this little clearing suck itself out of the world and show you everything you need to know. However. As I say, I have an appointment I'm reluctant to delay so we'll make it quick.'

I cast a glance at Schubert who frowns and nods at the ground. 'Mow wow,' he states and I shuffle uncomfortably. I fear I am outnumbered.

'Sit down,' commands Aggie and points behind me. I see a comfortable-looking cushion which I'm pretty sure wasn't there before and I lower my posterior into it. It is indeed a very comfortable cushion, but even as my bum is registering this, a little fire erupts between us, illuminating golden flecks in Aggie's eyes and rippling highlights through her cherry-wood hair.

'Fire. We've got the earth as we're standing on it, and we've got the air because we — or you — are breathing it. So now all *I* want is some water; and *you* don't need that silly altar you created and you certainly don't need a knobbly stick. You're using it like a crutch, my dear and you don't need it — just like how it was with brandy, for my dear Lord — ' Then she bites her lip and her cheeks turn the silvery-pink colour of mother-of pearl. 'Oh, I shouldn't divulge details.' And she smirks, knowingly, and I wonder if that's another man she slept with.

'Aggie, who is my great-great grand-father?' I ask sharply.

'A man who was very good to me,' she says, 'although his mother, the old crow, never approved. Said he was a playboy and sent him off all over Europe to keep him away from me.' She sniffed in disgust. 'But it didn't stop us and the subterfuge worked marvel-lously. Now lassie, let's get down to business.' I know I'm never going to find the answer out to that question, which is frustrating.

Aggie looks up to the sky again and holds her hand out. Somewhere, way above us, is a rumble of thunder and all of a sudden there's a little fluffy raincloud drifting in from a cluster of trees. It floats about shoulder height and settles near my glamorous great-great-granny. A few drops of rain tumble out of the cloud and she catches them in her palm and flicks them into the flames, murmuring something under her breath. The flame pulses violet and orange and it looks like a Bunsen burner.

'There you go, have a look. Tell me what you see. Now concentrate, mind,' says Aggie.

I stare into the flames and feel the warmth on my cheeks. I wonder vaguely if the combination of water and heat is going to make my hair frizz up even more, as it has apparently done with Schubert's fur. He now looks to be twice the size he actually is and appears to be quite proud of that fact.

'I can't see anything,' I say. 'It's just a pretty coloured fire.'

'No pictures? No messages?'

I squint. Sure enough, there are shapes appearing in the flames; shapes that are starting to look a little familiar. 'Oh. Oh, oh, *oh*. I can see my house.'

'That's a start. What else do you see? What do you see if you look closely? What do you *really* want to see? Think positively now, that's the *real* magic.'

I lean forward and peer into the flames. The shapes are bending and wavering, but I can definitely see the shape of the building Ewan and I live in.

'There are some shadows in the windows,' I say thoughtfully, 'like people, moving around.'

'That's good,' says Aggie. 'What else?'

'Gosh!' I say in delight. 'If I look very closely, I can see through my window!' In fact, I can definitely see a little me-shaped figure inside the building, and now I'm disappearing up the staircase to Ewan's flat. I wave at the me-shaped person and — 'Oh! I'm going up the stairs. I'm going to bump my head. I'm going to — oh!'

I see the me-shaped person pop up in Ewan's flat and then a Ewan-shaped person comes down some more stairs — from his DJ room, I assume — and meets the me-shape in Ewan's flat.

'I'm confused.' I pull a face and look

138

at Aggie. 'How am I moving around the house like that? Why am I climbing through the ceiling?' I look back into the flames and there's a Schubert-shape prowling around the rooftop, winding itself around the chimney pots, strutting his stuff in, I have to say, a very confident manner. As I watch, he manages to slip through a window with only a very small amount of inelegance as he doesn't quite make the leap the first time, and he disappears inside the house and pops up in the window where me and Ewan are, then begins to clean himself self-righteously.

'It's all your house,' Aggie says cryptically, and grins. 'You're all going to live there for a very long time. Listen. I wouldn't normally tell anyone this, but for you I'll make an exception.' She leans towards me and whispers some very odd stuff in my ear and eventually I sit back on my comfy cushion and stare at her. 'But first — ' she says, as my mind reels and churns like it's at an LSD induced ceilidh' — we need to make sure certain people are dealt with.'

'Certain people,' I repeat, still thinking of the things Aggie has said.

'Yes. They're in that car, you know, and we have to deal with them.' She makes an elegant gesture with her hand and the fire goes *poof* and then disappears. 'This is what I suggest you do.'

And she leans in towards me again and I wonder, with, I must admit, a little shivery thrill, what she's going to tell me now . . .

'You have to get up off your backside first, Nessa darling. Nobody likes a lazy witch.'

14

EWAN

'Nessa!' I'm pushing through the forest in the general direction she went, and although I know she'll complain and say she didn't need rescuing I can't let her just disappear into Kincladie Woods like that.

Kincladie is only about half a mile long and logically speaking she will come out the other side of it in about ten minutes if she runs in a straight line; but what if she doesn't? What if she stumbles and falls and hurts herself?

Okay, I'm probably being a bit melodramatic and the last thing I am is some sort of hero — but I care about her and I want her safe.

I love her and I want her safe.

The thought makes me stumble

instead and I shake it out of my mind.

'Nessa!' I try again. 'Nessa!' My voice is deadened with this fog and the tree canopy, but it doesn't stop me shouting.

It's ridiculously dark in here now and I'm forced to stop and fumble for my mobile phone. I manage to locate the torch app and turn it up to its full strength. I do a sweep around the area, and all I can see are bloody trees. There's a well-trodden pathway beneath my feet, so at least I've managed to stay on that but it's really cold now and I'm not seeing Nessa anywhere in the torch beam.

Then I notice a break in the trees before me, and head towards what seems to be a clearing. For a moment I worry that I'll walk into some scene of carnage there and I'll see eight women swinging from the tree branches up above me, but I tell myself not to be so stupid and I keep going across the uneven ground.

There's the briefest flicker of light in

the clearing, but it's enough to make me start running again and calling her name. I hope to God she's found that bloody cat and her torch app is working as well.

'Nessa!' I yell. 'Is that you?'

I jog into the clearing with my torch trained before me and thank God, I see her standing in the middle of the clearing holding that damn cat and blinking like an owl as the beam illuminates her fully.

'Nessa! You're okay! And you found Schubert? Thank God! Now I think we've seen enough of this place and we need to go back to Winnie. Deal?'

'Sort of,' she says. 'But I didn't need rescuing, you know. I'm fine.' She blinks again and looks a little vague. In fact, she's looking at me really strangely. 'But thank you, Ewan, for coming for me.'

There's an odd little awkward pause where nothing happens, then she takes a step towards me. She looks up at me and takes another step. Then I find myself taking a couple of steps towards her . . .

She feels so good in my arms and she fits so snugly, it makes me wonder why I didn't do this earlier. Her head is just about level with my chest and my chin rests on her hair if I just drop my head down a little.

Her voice is muffled, but not by the fog this time; it is muffled by cat and fleecy hooded jacket material and it sounds so lovely. 'Ewan, I very much want to do this for a very long time with you,' she says in that funny stilted way she has, 'but I'm afraid I have pressing business with the car in the verge and you have to come with me.'

'Okay,' I say, slightly bemused. 'I'm just glad I found you both before anything else did.'

'I'm fine,' she says.

And I think it's at that point where I realise that, with her arms full of beast, there is no way she could have been using the torch app on her mobile.

I pull her closer for a second or so

longer and look around us, my heart pounding just a little faster in my chest. A breeze whips past my legs and vanishes into the forest with a rustle of foliage — apart from that, there's nothing out of the ordinary here.

But I will be damn glad to get back to Winnie.

NESSA

Ewan might think I'm totally crazy, but I have to do this and I have to see whether Aggie was right. There's an awful lot at stake and I don't want to make any mess ups.

I haven't really been trained fully yet, so a lot of this is going to be instinct.

Ewan takes my hand ever so gently to lead me out of the clearing and back to the road. He's even shining his torch app out the front for us, but I really don't feel as if I need the light to show me the way out. I'm pretty certain I could lead *him* out of Kincladie and be none the worse for it.

I heft Schubert into a more comfortable position because I've only got one arm free to hold him and he appears to have lost all desire to walk.

Actually, I can't trust him not to run off again if I do put him down.

I wish I had brought his lead.

But there's something else that keeps bugging me, to be honest, apart from Schubert's indolence that is.

If Aggie is right about the car in the verge, then maybe I can allow myself to believe her when she says 'it' will happen between Ewan and I. I already know she is right about his rear end. So I know I need to get to that car and check it out. Then I can go from there.

But then I realise Ewan is talking. I think it's an act of bravado to show me how manly he is, and to hide the fact that Kincladie Woods is a very, very quiet place indeed in the late evening near Halloween.

'I definitely think these woods have something going on in them,' he says, stepping over a fallen log. 'I'm just not sure what it is yet. And I don't want to scare you by talking about it if you don't want to.'

I truly believe he thinks he is doing the right thing by not discussing the ghosts in this place.

So of course, because I'm an idiot, I have to shatter his illusions by letting him know I'm not a properly girly girl like Fern, who would be scared of the woods and would let him take the manly lead. No. I have to make a comment that just makes me sound like a whack-job.

'It's the Roman soldiers,' I tell him.

I don't think it's a coincidence when he stumbles, then suddenly stops and turns to stare at me. Even his torch app is wavering, as if to highlight the fact I am a truly non-girly-girl whack-job.

'*Sin. Dex. Sin. Dex*,' I say. 'You know?'

Clearly Ewan doesn't know. 'What?' he says. His voice is ever so faint.

'*Sin. Dex. Sin. Dex*,' I repeat. 'What

they say when they're marching. Yes? Didn't you hear them?' Then I think I should probably shut up but it's too late. It's like when we were in his flat and I told him all that other stuff.

He's so easy to talk to and I think that's the problem.

'Um, yes,' I continue, my voice as faint as Ewan's was. 'They marched right past me. Never mind. Come on. Let's go. Chop chop.' I pull at his hand, hoping he'll start off again and it's like pulling at a lump of granite.

'Ewan, were you a prop forward in rugby?' I ask him, just to be sure. I tug at him again and he remains immobile, just staring at me.

'No,' he says. 'I was a fly-half. Nessa? What the hell — '

'Shhhh!' I snap. 'Don't *say* that around here. The witches aren't here anymore, but it's the *principle* of the thing!'

'The witches?'

'Yes. Aggie said — '

'*Aggie?*'

'Oh dear. Oh my.' I improvise. 'Perhaps I stumbled and hit my head. Oh well. Let's go and find that car. Come on, Ewan.'

This time, he allows himself to be tugged along. Suddenly, I'm in the lead, taking us out of the woods. Ewan's torch wobbles again, then it steadies and he lifts it up and it's shining over my shoulder but I haven't the heart to tell him I really don't need it.

I think he thinks he's being helpful.

EWAN

Nessa pushes forward and Schubert is glaring at me over her shoulder. I try not to catch his eye and concentrate on lighting the way for Nessa. I wonder if she really has fallen over and hit her head — otherwise what she's saying doesn't make any sense at all.

Then I remember the funny feeling I had at the Maggie Wall monument and the whisper of a breeze that whipped past me in Kincladie Woods and I stop thinking because that way madness lies.

It doesn't take Nessa long to get us out of the woods and soon we are standing at the edge of the path and Winnie is there, looking awfully welcoming. I try to guide Nessa towards Winnie and back to some semblance of normality, but she pulls me towards the main road and heads along the path to where that car is parked. Then she stops and disconnects her hand from mine. My hand feels weird now she's no longer holding it — like it's missing something.

But that's soon rectified.

'Hold him,' she commands, and shoves Schubert into my arms. I stiffen, expecting the gargantuan creature to hiss and spit, but he snuggles into me and I find myself stroking him. We follow Nessa to the parked car.

She walks right up to the car and leans in towards the driving window; then she raps on the window with enough force to terrify anyone in there. 'Get out. Now!' she shouts.

I'm not surprised when nobody answers. If the inhabitants are persons of a weak constitution, then being confronted in their car beside a haunted wood just before Halloween is *not* going to make them get out of it. God knows, they might have died from a heart attack by now.

'Is that wise?' I ask. Nessa leans even further towards the window. From the inside she is going to look like some freakishly weird squashed-face person, which is definitely not going to encourage the driver to come out and tackle her.

She ignores me and addresses the window instead. 'I have a torch,' she yells. Then she thrusts her hand out and I guess that she wants my mobile. I manage to hand it over to her, encumbered as I am by cat, and she holds the phone right up against the glass. There is a cloudy circle on the window where she has been breathing and the outlines of two people huddled in the car.

'Have it your way then,' she says, and I can hardly believe my eyes when she raises her forefinger and begins to draw a pentacle in the vapour.

The passenger door suddenly flings wide open and a woman leaps out of it. She's shouting something, and it's pretty garbled, but I can pick up a few uncomplimentary phrases, mainly accusing Nessa of being a witch — or a bitch — it's hard to make it out — and also accusing her of something else:

'You've had your evil eyes on him *forever*,' the woman screeches, 'and you expect me to believe this wasn't *planned*? And *what* are you doing to the car? Is that going to make us crash and *die*? Will you be happy *then*? God, you're a foul, nasty, ugly little — '

'Good evening, Fern,' I say, and Fern seems to see me for the first time. She gawps at me and I sense the stream of vitriol will soon be directed to me. 'Fancy seeing you here,' I say, in order to stop her in her tracks — and also because yes, it is very odd to see her here.

'Nope. Not at all,' says Nessa, before Fern can respond. 'It won't make you crash and die. But I think you'll find your car won't start.'

At that point, the driver door swings open and it catches Nessa on the leg with a horrible crunch, throwing her off-balance.

'Ouch!' she says and sits down hard on the tarmac, banging her head on the wing mirror on the way down. The wing mirror shifts with the impact and the glass itself splinters.

'Hey!' I yell and run forward, ready to punch the nose of whoever did this to her. Well. I try to run. I sort of stagger due to the Beast; but then Schubert kind of tenses his muscles (I'm actually surprised to feel he has got muscles under that fur, but I definitely feel something tense up) and he springs out of my arms and is in the car before I can stop him.

There's a nasty few seconds of yowling and crashing and masculine swearing and then a man leaps out of the car, fending the cat off him. Schubert has turned into a fiendish mass of fur and teeth and talons and I do not pity the bloke beneath him.

I pity him even less when he finally throws the cat off and stands gasping at the side of the road. I can see by the car's courtesy light that it's the paparazzi reporter bloke from the paper — and God love him, he's all dressed in camouflage tonight. There are also quite a few holes in the clothing now, thanks to Schubert trying to rip the fabric to shreds.

'Get a tip off, did you?' I growl, and I'm a bit surprised to hear my voice come out like I've chewed a ton of gravel. I take a step towards him with my fist curled up ready to strike him and he cringes as if he knows what's coming; but Nessa raises her hand 'Stop!' she says, quite firmly.

It's so weird, because I automatically stop.

'But Nessa, he's hurt you.'

'I'm fine,' she replies and struggles to her feet. Then she kind of collapses again and whimpers, 'Ouch.' Then she shakes her head and holds her hand to her forehead. She pushes her hair out of the way and then looks down at her hand in some surprise.

'Well this wasn't meant to happen,' she says. There's blood on her fingers, dripping down from a nasty cut where she connected with the mirror.

Schubert makes a little whimpering sound and clambers up onto her knees. Then he licks her forehead. I can't quite help myself from recoiling at the thought of that whiskery little tuna-face so close to mine and the idea of that rough tongue dragging across my skin, but Nessa doesn't seem bothered.

'Thank you, Schubert. I'm fine now. Really fine. Thank you,' she says. She lowers her face and kisses him, then stands up again — more carefully this time — and I hurry over to help her. She must be feeling a bit fragile because she doesn't try to shake me off.

Then she turns and sees Fern.

Nessa narrows her eyes at her and points at her. It's rather Gothic, because some blood drips off her hand and she really does look like some medieval witch standing there with her black hair and her white face with the red streak across it. She's a little hunched up as well and all her weight is on her right side, so her left one must have really got a good bashing; if I didn't know her so well, I think I would be a little scared of her right now.

'I think you'll find — ' she says in a low voice ' — that the car will not start. Like I told you. Go on.' She lurches around to face the paparazzi guy, and points at him. 'Try it.'

'Load of — ' begins Fern, and Nessa whirls around to her as well, accompanied by a sort of reeling waddle as her weight shifts. I can see her face close up and it's all pinched and closed like it's really hurting her but I know she's not going to give them the satisfaction of seeing it.

The pap man doesn't need telling twice. He jumps in the car and turns the key. I can see that his hands are shaking. Fern is hanging onto the passenger door, clearly ready to jump inside and have him drive her off into the distance.

But the car won't start. It turns over and over and over.

But it will not start.

I cast a quick, shocked glance at Nessa and she looks quietly triumphant.

'Excellent,' she says. She looks at me and her eyes are shining in the light coming from inside the car. 'I wasn't sure about that, but it looks like I've succeeded.'

Suddenly, ditsy, loveable Nessa is back and that Gothic *Wuthering Heights* Nessa has vanished back into the haunted forest.

Gothic Nessa was kind of creepy, I have to say.

'Only one thing for it,' says Nessa. She turns back to the car and leans on the still-open driver's door. It's probably to give the impression of power and the fact that she is in charge, but I think it's more to do with the fact that her leg is hurting again and there's a fresh stream of blood coming from her head and she's probably going to pass out with it any second now if she doesn't support herself. 'Back to Winnie. I think we need to talk about this, don't we?'

Then very quietly and very elegantly, she slides down the passenger door and lies in a heap at the bottom of it with her eyes closed.

15

NESSA

I wake up in Winnie, wrapped in the hairy crocheted footstool cover and for a moment I can't remember what happened or why I'm here. Then Ewan's face swims into focus and I remember.

'Hey you,' he says.

'Hey you,' I say.

'Mow wow,' says Schubert.

'Hey Schubert,' I say.

'For God's sake, can we go now? She's not dead, so we can go, yeah?'

'Good evening Fern,' I say.

'Ignore her,' says Ewan. 'She was just as worried as we were. I didn't like seeing you flat out like that and she even suggested her friend here should give you the kiss of life.'

I'm not surprised she volunteered

Camo-Man rather than Ewan, but I'm not going to split hairs. I just wish I could remember being carried in Ewan's arms though, because I bet that happened and I bet, under other circumstances, I would have very much appreciated it.

My head is a little bit sore and the skin feels tight so I reach up to give it a prod. It seems as if someone found the first aid kit, because I've got a sticking plaster on the cut. Unfortunately, by the feel of it, it's one of those weird shaped sticking plasters that you put on heel injuries, so it probably looks a bit stupid but I don't really care right now.

'It was the biggest one in the box,' says Ewan frowning.

'That's fine. Thank you, Ewan.' I make to sit up and he rushes forward and helps me.

Fern makes a sound like a strangled fox. 'You should have taken her to A&E and left her there,' she says.

'How could I do that?' says Ewan coldly. 'We discussed it, remember?

Your friend's car isn't working and I don't know where the keys are for this one and there's no bloody mobile signal.'

'You got inside this thing, didn't you?' says Fern. 'Surely *that* key fits the ignition?'

'Winnie's back door doesn't lock,' I say. 'It would have been open. So no, that key wouldn't help. Because there *is* no key.'

'When will *my* car work?' whines Sticky. 'I want to go home.' He's all huddled in the corner, dressed in his awful grungy, shredded camouflage gear and clearly trying to get as far away as possible from Ewan and his fist.

'When I say it can,' I snap back. Sticky cowers again and licks his lips. I look at him and say, more kindly, 'what is your name, Mr Paparazzi Person? I don't like to keep calling you Sticky.'

Maybe he doesn't realise I call him that? Oh well. I have a head injury. I can plead confusion.

'Clarence,' he mutters. 'Clarence du Bois. That's my professional name.'

'Clarence Wood,' I say. 'Okay then, Clarence Wood. I won't sue you this time, but please feel free to tell me why you and her were stalking us? Oh, Ewan!' I turn and smile at Ewan. 'Isn't it funny how he's called Clarence Wood when we're near Kincladie Wood?'

'Shhh,' says Ewan. 'He can't help his name.'

'I have a head injury,' I say. 'Maybe that's why I find it funny. I didn't have a head injury before when I mentioned the ghosts. Just to clarify. Anyhoo.' I smile at Clarence Wood in what I hope is a friendly manner. 'Please tell us why you stalked us. And more to the point, how did you know where we were?'

Clarence is more than happy to talk. I think Schubert has taught me well. Go for the weakest link every time and you'll usually get an answer.

'I got a call from my source,' he begins.

'And that lady over there is your

source?' I ask, pointing at Fern. Schubert growls. 'I must say, I use that term loosely. Lady that is.'

'Yes. That lady is my source,' he says, nodding like one of those noddy dogs you get in the back of cars.

I must get a noddy dog for Winnie.

'And?' I say.

'And she said she had a feeling you were trespassing somewhere. You,' he says, waving his arm around encompassing me and Ewan Grainger — then, after a brief windmilly sort of movement, encompassing Schubert as well. 'You lot. She said she thought it was an historic monument in Perthshire, a listed building that nobody should be going near as it was on private land. And worse than that, she thought you were planning on defacing it and then you were going to those woods to destroy the evidence. She said it was because a rival author had written a successful book about it so you, Mr Grainger, needed to address that. And you, Miss McCreadie — or may I call you Agnes — ?'

If looks could kill the man would be a corpse.

'Okay, I guess I can't call you Agnes,' he says, shrinking into the corner even more. 'But as I was saying, you, Miss McCreadie, were aiding and abetting by erasing the trail so the police couldn't pin it on you when questions were asked. And after all, it's not really fitting behaviour for a famous author, Mr Grainger, Sir, so she thought you were being coerced in some fashion. We were here to protect your reputations.'

Now, I know I've suffered a head injury tonight, but when did we ever concoct a plan like that? And 'protect our reputations'? My foot. She would have made him plaster my photo on the front of the paper and have a pained picture of Ewan inside, saying I'd kidnapped him. '*Oh, oh, oh, my boyfriend got kidnapped by the mad marijuana lady who hates puppy dogs . . .*'

'Mr Clarence Wood. If you will

excuse me from saying this, you are, in fact, barmy,' I tell him, as kindly as I can. 'Ewan and myself — ' Schubert growls again, ' — and of course Schubert my cat, are here researching witches for Ewan's next novel. That's all there is to it, really. Ms . . . ummm . . . well, *her*, anyway, I've never bothered to learn her surname, would probably have hated it. I can't see her enjoying haunted woods and witchy monuments to be honest. And the three of us were very well-behaved. The man in the pub can vouch for us.'

'The *pub*?' bellows Fern, who is now a shade of puce. 'So you took her to the *pub* as well? For a *drink*?'

'No. For a meal,' I say. 'Unlike you, wine is not one of my five a day and anyway I paid because Ewan has made tea all day for us, so it was only fair.'

She chooses to ignore that, but goes for the jugular in another way. 'There's a lot of cars not starting around here, isn't there?' she hisses back. 'One of your many talents is it? Wrecking cars?'

'Not really. Mr Wood's car isn't wrecked. As you will see when it drives back home.' I choose to ignore the fact about Ewan's car not starting because that should never have been any of her business. 'But what I am interested in, is how you knew where to find us? Did you spy on Ewan? Did you have his phone chipped with GPS?' I challenge her.

'A GPS chip!' cries Ewan who has been very quiet and has been, I know, watching me with eyes as big as saucers. He drags his gaze to Fern with some difficulty. 'In my phone? Fern! Did you really do that?' He looks angry and shocked at the same time.

I thought only Schubert could do that expression, so this is a bit of a revelation to me.

'Of course I bloody didn't!' she says, crossing her arms and throwing herself back on the bench chair. I must wash that throw rug now she has sullied it. 'It was when I rang you and she was singing and shouting and *demanding* things. I did some research and found this place.' She leans forward again and flings her arms out wide. 'So sue me. You're my famous boyfriend and you're off with other women. What was I meant it do? Sit at home and let it happen? Seriously, Ewan, if you want me to get us some decent publicity with Vinnie and Jude, you're going to have to rein yourself in. We've got the potential to go even *further* and I can make that happen. God, I'll never get to meet Guy Ritchie if you blow this chance by messing on with *her*. You're becoming a loose cannon, Ewan. We have to stop it.'

'No,' says Ewan and his voice is low and a little dangerous.

Oh my. I really like his voice like that and it makes me go deliciously shivery in certain places.

'You were meant to trust me,' he says, still in that voice.

'*Trust* you?' she yells, breaking the spell. 'When you've been with her all day, and you've been to the *pub* and

you've been *pawing* each other?' Fern
has a habit, I have noticed, of
over-emphasising words.

'*Pawing* each other?' I cry, emulating
her. 'The only person pawing *anyone*
around here has been *Schubert*. We
have not been *pawing* each other all day
at *all*!'

Although God knows I've wanted to
paw Ewan Grainger for years, but that's
very different. I mentally run through
the physical contact we've actually had
today and it's all been very respectable
and innocent. There was that moment
in Kincladie when we hugged, and
when he rubbed my back when I was
dying from physical exertion after the
pub and I remember that we held
hands so as not to become separated in
the haunted woods. Not much really.
Oh, and the LuaLua moment. But that
hug in the forest was the nicest — and
if it wasn't for what Aggie had implied,
I wouldn't even have let that happen.

I know now that he's going to be
mine anyway, one day, so why shouldn't

I have helped things along a little back there?

'And I haven't even *seen* the tattoo on his shoulder!' I throw in for good measure, just to prove it to her.

Oh dear.

Maybe that wasn't *quite* the right thing to say.

16

EWAN

I really can't believe what I'm hearing Fern say. I have never been accused of anything like this in my life, and it's not going to happen now. God knows I've been faithful to her and yes, today has made me see what I'm maybe missing with Nessa, but I haven't done anything about it at all.

But you know what?

Famous boyfriend?

Is that what it all boils down to in the end? Me and Vinnie and Jude — and possibly Guy Ritchie — and Fern, just in there, just loving the spotlight?

I really wish I *had* done something about Nessa today. This has finally made me realise how false and stressful my relationship with Fern has become.

I'm not blaming Nessa at all. And

I'm not blaming myself, either. It's just I've had a sudden revelation and this is what has to happen. I can't be happy with Fern. I will never be happy with Fern. I think, without the film deal, it might have fizzled out anyway. She's pretty, no denying that — but it was never meant to last. We were never meant to go beyond those first few heady months were we? It was just easy to have her there, dealing with the media fallout, while I worked on screenplays and soundtracks and posed every so often for a photoshoot.

I've realised that I don't want my life planned out for me. If I plan anything at all, I want it to be planned with someone I care about and who cares about me — someone who doesn't care about how much money my latest book has made me and how good we look together in the gossip columns. And someone who doesn't care that we should eventually move to a better part of the town and who doesn't care about contacting *Yay!* and *Hiya!* magazines to film our 'perfect proposal' in the Caribbean.

I hate the idea of the Caribbean.

I hate the idea of proposing to Fern.

And I know for a fact she contacted those magazines because both editors rang me to get an exclusive.

'Fern, I have no idea where you got this impression from. Nessa is a friend. She came with me today because I thought she'd be interested in it all and I needed to get away from the whole imaginary club-scene thing and breathe some proper, fresh air. But you know something else? I've had a bloody good day with Nessa and I'm not about to let you spoil it. You're controlling and resentful and jealous and I don't think I can deal with that any more. I'm sorry, Fern, but I think you've just crossed the line and I don't really want to be with you any more.'

There now. I've said it, and it can't be unsaid. I'm waiting her for the thunder and the lightning and the sky falling down — but strangely nothing happens.

'Well now.' That's Nessa. She's sat up under that hairy rug and she is, in turn, staring at me and staring at Fern. 'I think you're being a little bit impulsive Ewan. It's one mistake. Is it enough to dump her over?'

'You keep out of it, you horrible little witch!' screams Fern. She leaps up from the bench seat — no mean feat in a crowded camper van — and looks as if she wants to punch someone. I stand up as well, because there is no way I'm letting her punch Nessa. If she wants to punch someone, she can punch me. Winnie lurches oddly with my movements, but I stand my ground.

'Fern. It's over,' I say. 'This has just proved to me how bad things are. The fact you felt you had to line up a reporter — '

'Investigative reporter,' interjects Clarence Wood. I'd completely forgotten he was there.

' — investigative reporter,' I continue, 'because you wanted some more coverage. And it's not the first time you've tried to get Nessa into trouble. Do I have to remind you of the drug incident? Or the nasty poster about Nessa outside the house? It's not on, Fern. It's not right. What's she ever done to you?'

'I. Just. Don't. Like. Her,' hisses Fern. 'Isn't that enough?'

'Have you *heard* yourself?' I say, incredulously. 'You don't even *know* her.'

'Stop sticking up for her!' yells Fern.

'No!' I yell back.

'Cup of tea, anyone?' trills Nessa. 'Please? Can we have one? To settle ourselves? Oh look, Schubert's sorting it out for us.'

The comment is so random that both Fern and I stop in our tracks and stare at the cat.

I can't believe it. He has nosed the top of the tea caddy off and, as we stare at him, he stares back and lifts a paw.

Then he tips the caddy over, and two tea bags fall onto the counter.

Schubert sits down and glowers at us. Then he glares at me and Nessa, and glares at the coffee jar.

'I think he wants us to have coffee, Ewan,' mutters Nessa. 'Look at him. I'm not going to go against his wishes. Are you?'

'No,' I say faintly. 'Not at all. But that's not the tea caddy I used earlier. Is it okay — ?'

Schubert hisses.

'He says that it's fine,' says Nessa in a low voice, the sort of voice you would use if you were in the wilderness and a wild animal was nearby. 'My brother Alfie has a degree in Nutritional Physics. He works in a health food shop. I do believe those are the teabags he gave me at a discounted rate. I've never had any. I put them in here because they smelled funny and I prefer normal tea. But any port in a storm, eh?'

I have never heard of Nutritional

Physics, but this is not the time to argue. At least we've covered all her brothers now.

'No. That tea will be fine, I'm sure,' I say, still staring at the cat. 'And I'm very happy to have coffee if Schubert thinks it's best'

'I cannot *believe* you are talking about *tea* when my life is just *crumbling* around me!' wails Fern.

Oh great, she has morphed into 'wronged partner' Fern. I've never really noticed how dramatic her speeches are, but now I have, I find that it's quite wearing.

'Get a grip!' says Clarence Wood from the corner. Again, I look at him in astonishment. 'I can't think of a better thing than a cup of tea right now. Hey!' he says with, I think, an attempt at humour, 'will the cat make the tea as well?'

'Don't be ridiculous,' says Nessa, her voice dripping sarcasm. 'He's a cat.'

I try and fail to hide a smile as Clarence licks his lips nervously, clearly wishing he hadn't suggested it.

Nessa compounds it all by saying, 'I wouldn't trust him not to overfill the kettle. He's never been that good with measurements and spatial awareness. Here, Schubert, let me do it.'

She struggles out of her fleecy cocoon and I take a step forwards to help her, but she looks me straight in the eye and says, 'Sit down, Ewan. I have to do this. It's important.'

I see a flash of Gothic Nessa there, in the pale face and the dried blood in her hairline and I decide it's best not to argue with her. I sit down as she suggests and watch her bustle about in the tiny kitchen area, supervised closely by Schubert.

'We haven't finished our discussion,' says Fern eventually.

'There's nothing left to discuss,' I tell her as the kettle whistles joyfully. 'I don't want to be with you. That's it. You're not going to change my mind.'

'But Ewan . . . ' she starts, and her voice has mutated into that awful girly whine that she uses when she wants her own way.

'Please. Just leave it. You got a reporter to chase me up here. I don't need that sort of thing.'

'Here's the first cup of tea,' says Nessa. She looks at Fern then looks at Clarence. Pointedly, I think, she gives the cup to Clarence. 'And here's the second,' she says, handing a cup to Fern with a look of distaste on her face. 'Please don't choke on it. I'd like you to, but it would create a Difficult Situation, so it's best just to drink the stuff. And no. I haven't poisoned it, it's ginger and something, it's herbal,' she says as Fern makes a big thing about sniffing the steam coming off it. 'I just don't want to be responsible for you two setting off into the night and being cold. It's a chilly night and a long drive home for you. I don't have any biscuits. Sorry.'

I know for a fact there is half a packet of chocolate Hobnobs left in the biscuit barrel, but don't mention it.

'Coffee, Ewan?' says Nessa, handing me a fat, blue cup. 'It's nice and strong. Two sugars and black, just the way you like it.' She smiles at me and takes the second to last cup on the counter before shuffling back to her bench seat.

The remaining cup on the counter is one of those giant coffee franchise ones that look like soup bowls, emblazoned with the logo of a well-known coffee chain, and I wonder briefly how she managed to smuggle it from the shop and into Winnie.

Then I see Schubert dip his tongue ever so delicately into it and my thoughts are consumed by the idea of a caffeinated cat and I no longer have room in my mind to ponder Nessa's possible kleptomaniac tendencies.

17

NESSA

At least I know now why she's here. Her and Clarence Wood. I can't quite believe the fact that she thinks Ewan and I were up to something. If I'd really wanted to push that, I've had plenty of opportunity at home. Why would I bring him to the countryside in a camper van in order to do that?

The answer, of course, is that there are fewer Fern-shaped distractions in the countryside. Fern is maybe thinking that is the case, but she's still managed to become a distraction, only I would never, never have thought that she could have done it in such an ingenious way.

You've got to give her credit for that one.

'Is your coffee nice?' I ask, peering at

Ewan through the steam coming out of my cup. He's chosen to sit next to me again, which is very nice, although there is a definite droop to his manly shoulders, which makes me quite sad to see.

'It's lovely. Thanks, Nessa,' he says. Poor Ewan. I think the fact he has apparently terminated his relationship with Fern has hit him quite hard. It's a huge decision and perhaps inside my camper van with an audience was not the best place to do it.

'She'll probably take you back if you ask her,' I whisper to him. 'Blame it on a crime of passion. That sort of thing.'

He looks at me in surprise. 'But I don't *want* her back,' he whispers. I realise the surprised expression on his perfect face is his own surprise being externalised.

'Are you sure?' I whisper.

'Quite sure,' he says.

I'm desperate to ask him who, if anyone, he wants instead, but I don't.

There's a strange little moment when

we look at each other and I think I know what the answer to that one would be, but I'm the first to look away. It's maybe not quite right to look like that at each other when Fern's in the van. I may be many things, but I'm not a bad person. I take the opportunity to check what Schubert is doing and I'm pleased to see he's looking remarkably relaxed for a cat who's just had a cup of coffee.

I look back at Ewan, to point out the fact that Schubert has somehow, swiftly and silently, crept into his carrier, retrieved Catnip and is now sitting on the bench licking him and cleaning him as if Catnip were a kitten.

But Ewan is staring at Clarence. 'Bloody hell!' he says. 'Will you look at that, Nessa McCreadie?'

My name sounds funny spoken like that, but I like it. I look over in the direction he is nodding his head and I think in passing that he looks like one of those solar flowers you see on windowsills — nod, nod, nod. With the same stultified expression on his face.

'Bloody hell!' I say. But in contrast to his shocked expression, I can't help but smile. 'Ahhhh, how lovely,' I say. 'Look at him!'

Clarence Wood is staring at Fern like a love-struck teenager. He is gawping at her and his tongue is practically hanging out. His tea has been drained and the empty cup dangles loosely from his fingers by the handle. It swings dangerously.

'I'll take that, Clarence Wood, thank you very much,' I say and lean across Ewan to grab the cup from him. Ewan feels lovely and warm as I lean across. He managed to get next to the heater which blows warm air out from under the window, which may be part of it, but I don't hurry getting back upright to my side of the bench seat. 'Oops, sorry,' I say, having to lean briefly on his thigh as I sit up.

Well, I don't *really* have to lean on his thigh, but it's nice to do it.

Ewan just shakes his head. 'Look at

him! Just *look* at him!'

Then I tilt my lips up to his ear. 'Look at *her*, Ewan,' I whisper.

'Bloody *hell*!' he says and makes to stand up.

I put my hand on his arm to stop him. 'No! Stop! *Look* at her!' I repeat.

Fern is staring at Clarence Wood and before our very eyes her expression changes from a twisted mask of utter dissatisfaction verging on a temper tantrum, to one which softens and relaxes as her eyes fix on Clarence Wood.

Clarence licks his lips which would kind of spoil the mood if it was me on the receiving end of it, but with her, Fern, her eyes widen and her pupils dilate.

Her own empty tea cup slips and dangles from her fingertips and I make one more leap across the man-mountain that is Ewan to grab it. 'Mine, I think,' I say and rescue it from certain doom.

'You know, I don't think I told you

how flattered I was that you'd invited me up here on such an important mission,' says Clarence. He runs his finger around the inside of his camouflage jacket collar as if he's building up heat somewhere inside him.

It must be the ginger that was in his tea.

'I don't think I told *you* how you were the only person I could trust this whole *time*,' says Fern, with a delicate tremble to her lips. A perfectly pear-shaped tear rolls down her cheek and I wonder cynically how many times she has practised that manoeuvre.

'I would do anything for you, Fern,' says Clarence.

'I know you would,' replies Fern, a catch in her voice. 'A lot of men wouldn't and I *do* so appreciate it.'

I *do* so want to stick two fingers down my throat and make vomiting noises but I do not.

'Fern, my dearest, are you ready to go now?' asks Clarence. He drags his dopey gaze away from her and looks at us. He smiles, a rather slack, sloppy sort of smile and blinks. 'Thank you for the tea. It's been an emotional evening, but I think it's all worked out,' he says.

I look at that mouth and my stomach churns a little thinking about how it's going to feel to Fern when she snogs him later. Because she is *so* clearly going to be doing that. I can tell.

'You're very welcome,' I say. 'Can we trust that no silly stories are going to be circulated?'

'You have my word,' says Clarence.

'Okay. Thank you, Clarence,' I say. 'Now, have a safe trip back and I really hope I don't see either of you again for quite a while. I mean that in the nicest possible way, of course.' I smile innocently at him and he nods.

There is a quick flash of hatred in Fern's expression, however, as she glances at me, but it's nothing I can't cope with, thank you very much.

'The car?' she says. 'Will it start now?' I can tell it's almost killed her to address me directly.

'It most certainly will,' I tell her.

'Good,' she says. But her attention is already sliding away from me. I know that she will have other things to think about tonight, and that becomes apparent when she looks at Clarence again. The hatred in her face melts away and she matches his dopey, smiley expression.

'Let's go, darling,' she says and stands up. She's a little wobbly on her feet, but she holds her hand out to him regardless and he stands up and takes it. 'Oh, and Ewan? Just post my belongings to me, will you? That would be helpful.'

Ewan just nods, apparently speechless.

'Coming through,' I mutter and bend my legs sideways as Clarence and Fern walk down the centre of the van and out the back like it's the aisle of a church and they're doing the wedding march. They never take their eyes off each other and I'm surprised they don't miss their footing and tumble into a messy, sweaty heap on the ground outside Winnie and just stay there doing whatever they are definitely going to do in the next B&B they see on the drive back. I would have to move them along if they were on the ground outside of Winnie, I really would.

'Well now,' I say when they've gone. 'Well. Now. I tell you one thing, Ewan Grainger, and that's the fact I would be willing to bet they stop at the first place with a bed they find on their way home. What an amazingly super-duper fast relationship that was. Ah well. More coffee?' I hold my empty cup up and smile at him invitingly.

My smile widens when I tilt my head on one side and hear the sweet sound of Clarence's car engine turning over and the throaty roar as they speed off into the night.

'Coffee?' says Ewan finally. 'Coffee? Yes. Yes I think I wouldn't mind a coffee, Nessa. Unless you'd prefer tea?'

'Hell no,' I say. 'I'm not drinking that stuff.'

18

EWAN

Nessa is pretty insistent that we have another cup of coffee. I don't know how many cups of coffee I can take, but I know she won't entertain us having that ginger stuff her brother gave her.

Nessa looks at the teabags in the caddy that Schubert seemingly opened and then leans her head in to sniff them. 'They still don't smell right,' she says, 'and I don't think they would taste that good. I'm not one for stuff like that. Seems a bit fancy to me.' She pulls a face, then puts the caddy back on the shelf at the very back. She picks up the cups Fern and Clarence used between her thumb and forefinger and puts them in the tiny sink. Then she squirts a ridiculous amount of bleach and washing up liquid into them.

I didn't do that well in chemistry, but I'm hoping there's no chance of an explosion or any likelihood of poisonous gases seeping into the air.

'Coffee's probably better anyway,' I say. 'It's a long drive back and it's getting pretty late.' Nessa falters while she spoons instant coffee into my mug but doesn't answer me immediately.

'Do you want to go straight back?' she asks. 'Just let me know before I boil this up again.' She taps the spoon against the kettle, which is vanilla-coloured and patterned with roses.

'Well. Not really,' I say carefully. 'I don't want to go back any time soon. It just seemed like the proper thing to say. I mean, with the bump to your head and everything. I don't know if I would even let you drive just yet. I'd have to do it and I can't imagine you being happy about me taking control of Winnie.' Even as I say all that, I know it's just an excuse. Somehow, I think she knows too.

'That's good,' she says, not looking at

190

me, 'because I don't want to go back either.'

'Mow wow,' says Schubert.

'And neither does Schubert,' Nessa translates. 'Are you all right about breaking up with Fern?' she asks. 'It happened a bit quickly. Like I said, don't be rash on one silly little incident.' She brings the coffee over to me and then sits down opposite with her own.

'It wasn't one silly little incident. It's been boiling up for a while now. I guess this was just the last straw. I mean, who in their right mind brings a newspaper reporter all the way up here to try and catch their partner out?'

The more I think about it, the more ridiculous it is.

'It would have been different,' says Nessa, 'if anything was going on. But as far as I was concerned, we came up as friends. You had a girlfriend. Well, you had a girlfriend this morning. I don't think you have one now, do you?'

I can't help laughing. 'No,' I say, 'I

don't have one now.'

'That's good,' says Nessa. I shoot a glance at her, but she's got her eyes lowered and her nose buried in her coffee cup.

'Do you know something, Nessa?' I ask suddenly. 'I never even asked you if you had any better offers this weekend. God, I'm so sorry. I've dragged you into the mess that was my relationship and for all I know, you've got someone waiting anxiously to hear if you're okay and who wants to see you tomorrow — like a new boyfriend or somebody. And we're stuck here.' As I speak, though, I recall that I've never seen any potential boyfriends come through our joint front door, just a varying collection of indistinguishable McCreadie brothers that look a lot like Nessa. Apart from her family's fleeting visits, it's always been just Nessa and her cat. I doubt that this weekend would be any different, but I still feel bad, just in case.

'I haven't planned to see anyone else

tomorrow, and you know I haven't got a boyfriend,' says Nessa. 'But thanks for checking. I didn't need to have a random boyfriend anyway. I was waiting for the right person to come along.' She shrugs, her hands still around her coffee cup, but she won't look at me. 'Or at least I was waiting for him to be free.'

My heart does a little lurch and I look at her. She still doesn't meet my eyes — she's staring at something on the floor down past my ankle.

'Really?' I ask.

'Yep,' she says.

The atmosphere has somehow shifted and I think I know why my emotions have been so crazy today. And not just today.

They've been crazy every time I've seen her for the last three years; every time I've thought about her. Every time I've spoken to her. I couldn't wait to spend the day with her and I don't want to go home and not have her there. It's finally time to admit it.

It's her, isn't it?

She's the one I should be with.

It's always been her.

'Nessa — '

'Ewan — '

We both speak at the same time and before I know it, the coffee cups are on the floor and Nessa is in my arms and we're holding each other properly and kissing each other. And I know that it's exactly what I've wanted to do for years. And it feels good.

'God, Nessa. I'm so sorry, I'm so sorry,' I murmur between kisses. 'I'm so sorry. I should have realised. I'm sorry.'

'That's fine. You just had a different plan for a while. I'm pleased you haven't got that plan any more. I'm very, very pleased and what I said earlier is right. I'm very happy doing this and I want to do it for a very long time.'

Her words are also punctuated by my kisses and thank God these bunks convert into a double bed because for once I kind of know what's going to happen next and I certainly didn't plan it. But she doesn't seem to be objecting.

Maybe she planned it?

Ah, hell. Who cares?

I love Nessa McCreadie. There. I've admitted it *properly* now.

'I love you, Nessa McCreadie,' I say.

'I love you too, Ewan Grainger,' she replies and I know in a moment things are going to escalate sky high.

'But what about Schubert?' I say, remembering the all-seeing eyes of half a ton of cat.

'He's gone out the cat flap, he's fine,' she says. 'I unlocked it earlier.'

And then I don't worry about Schubert any more.

But I briefly wonder why she never mentioned the cat flap at all before now.

Nessa will always be full of surprises.

I'm quite looking forward to being surprised for a very long time.

19

NESSA

The drive home today is very different from the drive up here yesterday.

Today, I feel like I've achieved something, which is a very nice feeling. Even nicer than that, was the feeling I had when I woke up with Ewan. Yes, it was a wee bit chilly in Winnie this morning, but I have plenty of rugs and woollen blankets, so we were nice and cosy.

It was also nice to lie there all cocooned in said blankets with Schubert and Catnip reclining on my feet and watch Ewan make us all breakfast. I'm so pleased I thought to bring extra milk and fresh bread and butter and honey and cereal with me. Fancy that. And I got an excellent view of Ewan's tattoo as he stood there over the toaster with very little on. His tattoo is one of those Celtic crosses entwined with roses and a skull. It's really, really sexy and obviously part of his DJ alter-ego.

I'd caught sight of the tattoo as he came out of the tiny shower room as well. He was pretty surprised to be told that the shower room was there, but I think he enjoyed the shower, even though I had used most of the hot water beforehand.

Ewan doesn't seem to feel the cold as I do.

But anyway, I know that I have much to thank Aggie for; and there is also something I need to ask Alfie about as well, next time I see him.

Ewan's voice interrupts my deliciously wicked thoughts — thoughts in which his tattoo plays a major part — as we drive through the countryside. 'I'm not going to have your four brothers after me for keeping you out all night, am I?' he asks. I'm not quite sure if he is fully joking as he looks a little concerned.

'Oh no,' I reassure him, 'they'll be very happy for me. They know what it's been like for the last few years and have told me to get a wiggle on, on more than one occasion. Especially Alfie. He feels it the most, I think, being my twin.'

'Your *twin*?' repeats Ewan. Then he laughs. 'Nessa, don't ever stop being yourself, eh? You're going to keep surprising me for the rest of your life, aren't you?'

'And beyond,' I tell him, quite seriously. 'I'll haunt you, don't you worry about that.'

Ewan laughs and shakes his head. I don't think he believes me, but it's true. Aggie told me. But it won't be for years and years and years yet. We've got an awful lot of living to do first and several babies to have as well.

'I think it's about time I put you right on something first, though,' I tell him, feeling the need to be honest. 'Last night, when I was in the forest, I really did see Aggie — and the Roman soldiers. Aggie told me lots of things and I saw a few things too. It was Aggie who gave an indication of what might happen with Fern. She said if everything was to work out as it should, I had to have faith in my powers and do the car thing.'

'The car thing?' Ewan asks. 'What, when it broke down?'

'Yes. She said there was an awful lot to be said for positive thinking, so I thought positively and it worked.' I risk a glance at him and see that he is staring at me with his mouth slightly open in disbelief. I try not to think about what that mouth did to me last night, but fail and swerve slightly on the narrow roads back towards Edinburgh.

Ewan leans over and grabs the wheel, straightening Winnie up, but he still looks confounded.

I pull myself together and continue. 'So when the car failed to start, I knew she was right. And I knew that everything else she told me would happen. It was just a matter of time.' I smile. 'Luckily, I didn't have to wait long for it to happen.'

'But what about Fern and Clarence falling for each other?' asks Ewan. 'She couldn't have predicted that, surely?'

'No, but when Schubert made me use those tea bags, I knew he was in on the plan too. He knows Aggie, you know. I wonder if familiars can reincarnate?'

The thought sends me swerving towards another verge until Ewan grabs the wheel again.

'But the tea bags . . . ' he says, leaving the sentence unfinished.

'A nice touch weren't they? That was definitely Alfie. I do need to see him about that. It's made me wonder whether, if I have powers, then with him being my twin, whether he has them too, but he knew about it already.'

'I see,' says Ewan. But I don't know if he does really.

Ewan looks adorable when he's discombobulated.

'Anyway, I don't need my wand

anymore. Aggie says I don't need a knobbly old stick to work magic, I just need to believe in myself. And she suggested I dismantle my altar at work as well.'

'What, in case it generates evil or something?' asks Ewan, and I'm not *too* sure whether he's being facetious or just trying to understand.

'No. Don't be silly, Ewan. It's Wicca, it's not the Dark Arts. No. Aggie said a tidy desk was the sign of a tidy mind and anyway Mr Hogarth might get a bit worried if he comes into the office and finds me mumbling into a plant pot. And so,' I say frowning, 'might the clients. Oh well. But you know, having thought about it, there are a few things that have happened recently that I've wished for . . . '

I raise one hand from the wheel and count the wishes off, holding my fingers up in front of Ewan as and when necessary. 'I wished that Sticky would go after Fern instead of me, and he's gone after her *big* time. I wished we could spin out yesterday longer and we did. I wished — well, I wished that certain *things* might happen in the camper van last night.' I blush. 'And they did.'

'Several times,' adds Ewan, and I can tell he has a knowing grin on his face.

'Several times,' I agree. 'But there was other stuff that *didn't* happen.'

'Mow wow,' comes the aggrieved voice from the cat carrier in the back.

'Yes. I wished Schubert wasn't so opinionated, but I'm fine with that, really I am. It's what makes him special. But the important stuff happened. And I'm happy with that. Are you happy, Ewan Grainger?'

'I am indeed, Nessa McCreadie,' he says. 'At last, I am. And it's all because of you.'

I am very glad that he seems to have accepted the fact I'm a little strange and most probably a fledgling witch.

I nod, confidently. 'Aggie said you would be happy. I'm glad.'

'But can I ask just one thing?' he

says tentatively. 'Something that's been turning over in my mind for a little while? Or at least since last night.'

'You may,' I say.

'When my car didn't start yesterday morning, was that magic as well?'

I grin.

'Of course not, Ewan. That was purely mechanical. I've got the bits in my flat. You can have them when we get home.'

'Wonderful, marvellous girl,' he says, reverently.

And he lifts the hair from the back of my neck and kisses me on the nape, which almost makes me swerve into the verge again.

But it's worth it.

Good Lord, it so is.

20

NESSA

Some Months Later . . .

I'm still on a bit of a high and it's now March — it's almost the Spring Equinox, or as it's also known, the Vernal equinox or even 'Ostara'. At Christmas, I lit a candle for Aggie, because if it wasn't for her, things might have been very different.

I thought that Aggie might have liked the proper Winter Solstice marked in some way as well, so I made a beautiful, natural wooden Yule log and we burnt it in the garden. We've taken the fence down between mine and Ewan's gardens now, so it's a lovely little area and Schubert enjoys promenading around it with Catnip.

I heard that Fern and Clarence Wood

are engaged, so that at least means she's got something else to focus on apart from me.

And Ewan and I are both very, very happy about that.

Still, it wouldn't have been like Fern to not orchestrate one last little parting shot and spread a few unholy details around about me.

Ding dong. Ah, and I bet this will be something to do with it.

'Yes?' I say, opening the door to yet another worried looking girl.

'You're the witch, yes?' she says, twisting her hands in the hem of her coat. This one, then, is Eastern European. She has a delightful accent.

'Yes,' I say.

'You help me? I think there is a curse on me. I cannot make the man I love want me back.' She dabs the corner of her eyes with a white handkerchief and I make a clucking sort of sympathetic sound.

'Oh dear,' I say, and I mutter the only Gaelic phrase I know, whilst waving my hand over her and liberally sprinkling a bit of glitter in her hair.

The girl cheers up immediately and hands over a fiver. 'Oh thank you', she says. 'Will he love me back now?'

She spits a bit of misdirected glitter out of her mouth and I wait politely until she's finished spitting, then I speak. 'If he will not love you back,' I say sagely, 'a new man will be in your life soon and he will be better.'

'You are very kind,' she says and practically skips away from my doorstep. I shut the door and pop the fiver into a big jar that once held cat treats. When the jar is full, I shall donate it to the local cat rescue shelter place. It shouldn't be long now. Schubert wanders through with Catnip in his mouth and addresses the treat jar. This is no mean feat with the toy in his mouth.

'Mow wow?' he asks it quizzically yet muffled-ly.

'I know. It won't be long,' I tell him and stoop down to rub the sweet spot between his ears he loves so much. 'We could get you a friend when we're there. How would you like that?'

'Mow wow,' he says, thinking about it.

I open my mouth to respond, and there is an almighty crash from my lounge. Schubert goes into orbit and I swear and run into the room. I choke on the dust and dirt and bits of plaster that are now littering my lounge. There is a roar like an air-raid siren from downstairs because the noise must have woken the baby up, so I swear again.

I didn't know my hippie neighbour was pregnant. The kaftan hid a lot. I only found out when I saw them one day in the yard. The baby was screaming with all the power of a fair set of lungs and Rickie (that's his name. She's called Nickee with two e's) was staring at the baby — Zachary Rainbow Starchild — with a really bamboozled expression on his face.

I got an image of Aggie and found myself suggesting lavender to calm him down and something herbal they could use for colic as well.

It must have worked. I found a bowl of homemade lentil soup on my doorstep and some delicious cookies that quite cheered Ewan and I up that night.

Anyway, over the sound of Zachary Rainbow Starchild screaming and Schubert having hysterics and lying flat on top of Catnip to protect him, an apparition appears from the rubble. It's grey and white and groaning. It reaches its hands out and lurches towards me like a zombie.

I wonder if there's room for me under the protection of Schubert's paws.

Then I realise there is a damn big Ewan-shaped hole in my ceiling.

'It didn't go to plan!' moans the zombie. 'I fell through it!'

'Ewan Grainger!' I say, and stand facing the zombie with my hands on my hips. 'Why can you not use the front door like a normal person? I shall have to sleep in Winnie tonight. Or in your flat.'

'Mine,' he says. 'Sleep in mine. God, I'm so sorry Nessa. I thought I'd live a little dangerously and break a hole through the floor to your house. It would make it easier for us, you know. But it fell through a bit. Did I spoil anything?' He looks back over his shoulder in a slightly dazed fashion and I follow his gaze. My pot plants are scattered all over the place and the state of my books would make a librarian cry.

'You spoiled my pot plants and books,' I tell him. 'Look.'

'It was just meant to be a little hole,' he says, and makes a little square with the forefinger and thumb of each hand as if to demonstrate. 'I had a plan, you see — ' he says, but I cut him off by raising my hand in a 'talk to the hand' gesture.

'A plan,' I say. 'What have we said about plans?'

'You'll like this one,' he says and

lurches forward a bit more. I have a six foot three plaster-covered zombie heading towards me in my own lounge and it's rather incredible.

Then I realise the zombie is wearing nothing more than a pair of jogging pants and he doesn't even have socks on. I can see all of his muscles on his chest defined by the plaster dust and . . . mmmm. It's a very sexy zombie, actually. Plaster dust suits him disturbingly well.

'Don't you want to hear it?' he says and comes closer to me. Then he puts his filthy dirty arms around me and I start thinking filthy dirty thoughts.

'Mmm?' I say, nuzzling into his chest.

'I thought we could convert our flats back to how they were when they were a house. Then when the Happy Valley Munchkins leave next month, we could buy the lease from the landlord and convert the whole house back to one big place.'

'Are Rickie and Nickee and Zach

leaving then?' I ask, startled by this revelation.

Ewan nods. 'Yes. They decided that they wanted to move to Glastonbury as it wasn't as far to travel with a baby when they go to the festival.'

There is a weird sort of logic in there — no doubt a marijuana-induced sort of logic — but I let it go.

'How do you know?' I ask.

'The landlord told me,' he said.

'Ah, Mr Hogarth.' I nodded. 'You know, he's always spoken very highly of you and your police type family. He seems to be a very nice godfather to possess. You're a very lucky godson, Ewan, to have Mr Hogarth in your life.'

'See, you were *meant* to work for him, weren't you? Meant to move in here. Somebody else planned it all — even if you didn't. Because otherwise, we might not have met.'

'Oh we would have met,' I say, nodding. 'I'm certain about that. Especially if Aggie had anything to do with it. She's a strange one, she is.'

'She's incredible,' says Ewan and pulls me closer. 'Does that sound like a good plan, then? Or is it too 'planned' for you?'

'Oh no. I *like* this plan,' I tell him. 'I love you, Ewan. You know that don't you?'

'I do,' he says. 'And I love you too, Agnes McCreadie.'

And I don't even mind that he's calling me Agnes, because he's kissing me and it's ever so nice.

And I also know for certain that Schubert agrees with everything we've just talked about. He's a lovely cat, even though he's a little opinionated at times. But you know what — he's jolly well worth it.

And then I remember — ages ago, I had that other wish about having the basement as a workspace.

How marvellous!

It must be the power of positive thinking. I'll now be able to use the workspace for . . . something. Maybe I can set up a witchy consultancy or something.

'Mow wow?' suggests Schubert.

'That's a good idea, Schubert,' I tell him, impressed at his logic.

'Mow wow,' he agrees complacently.

And he licks Catnip.

Thank You

Thank you for reading *Every Witch Way*. I hope you enjoyed Nessa, Ewan — and Schubert's — story as much as I enjoyed writing it. It's a bit different from my usual work, and it's the first romantic comedy I've done, but sometimes it's good to jump out of the box and just go for it! I loved writing this novella and some of the words still make me smile when I re-read them. I don't know if 'doing edits' is meant to be such fun, but with *Every Witch Way*, it definitely was for me!

But all authors, in whatever genre they write, really value their readers as well-without you, we just have words on a page that mean very little. The road to publication is wonderful and if an author knows readers are enjoying their work, it's a fantastic feeling. It's even more special if people take the trouble

to leave a review. It's lovely to hear what readers
think and we all value their feedback.
If you have time therefore, something as simple as a one-line review on Amazon, a note on a book review site such as Goodreads or indeed a comment on any online store would
be hugely appreciated.
Please do feel free to contact me anytime.

www.twitter.com/kirsty_ferry
http://www.facebook.com/
kirsty.ferry.author/

I very much hope that you'll enjoy my other books as well.
Happy reading, and again, a huge thank you!
Lots of love
Kirsty
Xxx

We do hope that you have enjoyed reading this large print book.

Did you know that all of our titles are available for purchase?

We publish a wide range of high quality large print books including:
Romances, Mysteries, Classics
General Fiction
Non Fiction and Westerns

Special interest titles available in large print are:
The Little Oxford Dictionary
Music Book, Song Book
Hymn Book, Service Book

Also available from us courtesy of Oxford University Press:
Young Readers' Dictionary
(large print edition)
Young Readers' Thesaurus
(large print edition)

For further information or a free brochure, please contact us at:
Ulverscroft Large Print Books Ltd.,
The Green, Bradgate Road, Anstey,
Leicester, LE7 7FU, England.
Tel: (00 44) **0116 236 4325**
Fax: (00 44) **0116 234 0205**

*Other titles in the
Linford Romance Library:*

THE RIGHT MR WRONG

Pat Posner

When Tiphanie tells her boyfriend Howard she'll have to cancel their holiday to go and help her brother look after their niece and nephew, the consequences are catastrophic. Reeling from the breakup, Tiphanie arrives at her brother's home in a beautiful area close to the salt marshes, anticipating just a little peace and quiet. But any such hopes are dashed thanks to inconvenient feline escapades, a couple of very lively children, and her rather irksome — yet gorgeous — neighbour Kyle . . .

FINDING THEIR WAY

Angela Britnell

Attempting to shake off writer's block, novelist Fran Miller comes to the Cornish village of Tresidder to spend the summer with her long-time best friend, Lucy. She definitely isn't looking for romance, especially after a painful breakup with her last boyfriend — but it finds her nevertheless in the form of Charlie Boscawen, local baker and heartthrob. Soon she is being wooed with the most tempting confections imaginable. But Charlie has problems of his own . . . and what will happen when the summer comes to an end?

FINDING ALICE

Sarah Purdue

Evie Spencer has always lived life cautiously, wary of trusting anyone other than her beloved younger sister Alice, a talented painter who is studying art in Rome. Then Alice suddenly disappears — and Evie, determined to find her, must throw caution to the winds. Inexplicably stymied by the British Embassy, Evie is frustrated and desperate . . . until the mysterious Tom De Santis offers assistance. But there is more to him than meets the eye. Can Evie trust him, and succeed in finding Alice?

DOCTOR'S DESTINY

Phyllis Mallett

Having lost her husband and daughter in a boating accident, Dr Amy Merrill lives with her aunt and uncle and works at the local hospital. Still struggling after three years to put the past behind her, she befriends a young patient, Jane, brought to the hospital with pneumonia. Jane, she discovers, has run away from her rich father's house to search for her lost mother. And when Amy meets the father, handsome Grady Gilmour, her life will never be the same again . . .

A QUESTION OF THYME

Jan Jones

When Jen answers an advertisement to create a 1915 herb garden for a TV documentary, she expects it to get her out of a money hole, not to change her life . . . Borderline recluse Theo Grainger is scarred mentally and physically from an appalling fall seven years ago. Adjusting to the presence of a TV documentary team next door is one thing. Dealing with Jen Matlock, who helps people in trouble whether they want her to or not, is something else entirely . . .

BROUGHT TO ACCOUNT

Paula Williams

When Lauren Chapman is 'let go' from her job at a greengrocer's, her boss encourages her to take a position with a local accountancy firm, Northcott and Company. She does so reluctantly — but when the owner of the company is attacked and left for dead in his office, Lauren is the first person to find him. How is her late mother involved in the mystery? And will a budding romance blossom between her and handsome co-worker Conor Maguire — or is he trying to hide his part in the crime?